Demented

To Brooke,
Thanks! Enjoy!

Demented

Sarah J Dhue

Inspired by Dementium II

Original artwork by Ellie Taylor

Sarah J Dhue
2017

Copyright © 2017 by Sarah J Dhue

All rights reserved.

Cover design © Sarah J Dhue

Cover and interior illustrations © Ellie Taylor

About the Author photo © Audrey Parsell

This is a work of fiction. Names, characters, businesses, places, events and incidents are either the products of the author's imagination or used in a fictitious manner.

References to characters or locations from Dementium™ and Dementium II™ are

© Infitizmo LLC 2007-2017 and are used with permission for the sole purposes of this publication. All rights reserved.

First Printing: 2017

ISBN 978-1-387-36729-0

Sarah J Dhue

www.sarahjdhuephotos.com

Dedication

To everyone behind the Nintendo DS game, <u>Dementium II</u>, which inspired this book. And a very special thank you to Gregg Hargrove for being a simply delightful person to work with and giving me the green light to publish.

I would also like to thank my family for their support and help with the final draft, as well as my friends Dree and Nicole for helping me review and revise the first drafts.

A huge thanks to Ellie Taylor for the fantastic illustrations featured in this book.

This book would not have been possible without all of you!

To Dad – for introducing me to the Dementium games; finally made it to print. I love you and miss you every day.

Table of Contents

Preface...7

Part 1: Welcome to Pelf........................11

Part 2: It's Spreading..........................89

Part 3: The Plane of Anguish..................151

Part 4: It's Always Darkest Before Dawn....171

Epilogue: William.................................207

Preface

Back in 2008, Nintendo released a first person horror shooter game for the DS titled *Dementium: The Ward*. It was a bit of an anomaly, due to the fact that first person shooters were not really what the DS gameplay was geared towards. Nevertheless, the game was a great success, and two years later in 2010 they released the sequel: *Dementium II*. I had loved *Dementium: The Ward*, so I dove right into *II*. Not only were the gameplay and graphics much smoother, the story drew me even more than the first game. As I found notes and other remnants of those who had been in the asylum – Bright Dawn Medical Treatment Center – before the shit hit the fan, my imagination began to run wild and I wanted to piece together what had happened before the carnage I was witnessing in the game; who were these people?

Summer of 2010, I was sixteen years old and had just completed the first draft of my first complete novella, *For Two Cold Minutes*. Freshly motivated due to completing this milestone project, and inspired by the intrigue I felt from *Dementium II*, in 2011 I started a novel inspired by the game titled *Demented*. I wanted to write it as a four part novel, chronicling who the people were and what had happened leading up to the fateful moment when all Hell broke loose at Bright Dawn, and then write about the following events which took place in the game, taking some creative liberties of course.

When I write fan-fiction, I intensely study my source content; I played through the game a million times, taking notes and articles verbatim and plugging them into the book as dialogue, notes passed between characters, or book/article snippets. I took the names featured in these notes, articles, and signs, and fleshed them out into characters, adding a few of my own where needed. The monsters were my biggest challenge – I am not typically so much of a monster horror writer. I worked on the project off and on for the next few years and finally finished the first draft in 2013 during my second semester of college.

    I was actually really happy with what I had written – I had just recently started looking into self-publishing and was champing at the bit to unleash my creative work on the world. I edited a few drafts with the help of a few friends; another friend of mine actually drew seventeen original drawings of the monsters and sigils for me. Then I took a crazy scary plunge for a first-time-published indie writer of twenty years old: I sent an email to the developers of the game at Renegade Kid. It was a really polished and professional email expressing my love for the game, how it inspired me, and hoping that they would be willing to look over my draft and potentially give me permission to publish. I waited and… heard nothing back. I was not too discouraged and tried again after a few months had passed. Then I got discouraged and set it to the side for a while, and focused on what ended up being my next two books: *Eyes of Jade* and *The Legend of Sleepy Hollow*.

    A little over a year later – some time in 2015 – I was feeling brazen and tried again. Still no reply, which was saddening, but okay since I was on the fast track to publishing my first short story collection and attempt my first NaNoWriMo (National Novel Writing Month). I published the collection – *Timor: Volume I* – and got my 50,009 words for NaNoWriMo, which I continued writing. It became my first full-length novel, *Monsters*.

Summer of 2017 came around and, *Monsters* was doing pretty well. I decided to really put myself out there and see if I could secure a spot for it on the Lulu table at The Miami Book Fair 2017: an international event where my book would have the potential to be seen by over 200,000 book lovers. I started a GoFundMe, and between that and working very hard, I secured my place in the fair, as well as plane tickets for my family and me to attend. One night after securing my place in the book fair, I was feeling nostalgic – thinking of how far I've come as a writer and how far I still have to look forward to going with my writing career. I decided to visit one of the *Dementium II* developer's Twitter account and see what he was currently up to. And that was when I saw in his bio that it said "former Renegade Kid."

My eyes just about popped out of my head. "Former!?" I went to renegadekid.com and found out that the company had been amicably dissolved and the rights to the games had been split between developers based on the focus of each of their new individual developing styles. And it turned out that the developer I knew less about held the rights to the *Dementium* series. With a new swell of hope – but yet a bit of cynicism – I went to the website for Infitizmo Games, headed by the former Renegade Kid developer Gregg Hargrove. I went to the Contact page and inserted my query letter.

Then I hit send... and the screen went white. As a Web student, this made my heart drop. However, I decided to give it a few days and see if I heard anything back. When I did not receive any correspondence, I tried again and was once again greeted by a white screen. This led me to believe the Contact page was experiencing an error and, I was thrilled to see a Facebook Page linked to the main site. I clicked the icon, sent Infitizmo a message via Messenger, and waited.

Within a few hours, I had a very enthusiastic reply from Gregg. He was thrilled that the game had had such an impact on me and he had been thinking of featuring fan-inspired works on his website. He – of course – wanted to read over the draft to make sure it didn't really violate any canons within the universe and that it was not just awful. I sent him the draft, reference files, illustrations, and cover art. Our collaboration began! Over the next few months we kept in contact – both very busy with our own business as well as the collaboration. It was about a month into our correspondence when he said, "You're a good writer. I'm enjoying it so far," that I was like, "OMG, this is really happening!" Fast forward another month to late October 2017 and I had the green light to publish. I began right away on the final polish with the aim to publish in November.

And here we are: you are holding this book in your hands, about to embark on a journey six years in the making. I sincerely hope you enjoy this as much as I enjoyed writing it.

Part 1: Welcome to Pelf

Chapter 1

"Just make sure you stay on the pain medication for another five days and you should be all right," Dr. Nate Grimfield told the patient, scribbling something on his clipboard. He was young for a doctor, with wild blonde hair and bright blue eyes. It was the last day of his doctor internship at London General Hospital.

He walked out of the room and was headed to his 'office' - a glorified janitor's closet - when his friend, Mark Greer, yelled his name down the hall. "Nate!"

He turned, "What?"

"There's a letter for you. Looks official." He raised his eyebrows.

Nate rolled his eyes; Mark had a tendency to be sarcastic. All the same, Nate followed him to the lounge. Upon entering, Mark motioned to the table where he had set the letter. Nate picked it up. It *did* look official. It was stamped with an ornate seal, the return address to Michigan, USA. He opened and unfolded the letter. When he saw the letterhead, he felt a chill run down his spine and the letter slipped through his now limp fingers to the floor.

"What? What is it!?" Mark asked excitedly.

Nate sat down, propping his arm up on the table and resting his face in his hand. "It's a letter from Bright Dawn Medical Treatment Center," he said in astonishment, "over in the States."

"Why does that name sound familiar-" Mark's eyes suddenly bulged in recognition. "Crikey!" he shouted excitedly. Nate sat there another moment in disbelief. "Well, what's it say!?" Mark asked eagerly, bouncing on the balls of his feet.

Nate bent down and picked the letter up from the floor. He read aloud:

"Dr. Nate Grimfield,

Greetings from Bright Dawn Medical Treatment Center. Here at Bright Dawn, our staff comes from the best schools around the world. They are expected to take personal interest in their patients to ensure intimate and successful care. Many of the patients here are in some way psychologically disturbed, many even ranked among the criminally insane. However, in addition to the number of qualified doctors and nurses, we have a highly trained security staff for everyone's protection. Since Bright Dawn began in 1922, we have been paving the way for psychiatric care and cures. Our board of directors has taken a special interest in you and would like to offer you a position here at Bright Dawn. We would appreciate hearing from you soon.

With much expectation, Dr. Morris P. Richardson"

They both fell silent for a moment, the only sounds the buzzing fluorescent lights overhead and the soda machine cycling to keep its contents cold.

"We gotta tell the boss!" Mark suddenly cried, snatching the letter from Nate's hand.

Nate stood, and in one quick motion grabbed the collar of Mark's white lab coat and plucked the letter from his hand. "*I* will tell him."

Mark's shoulders slumped in disappointment as Nate passed him and made his way to the head doctor's office. He knocked on the door.

"Come in," rang the aged voice of Dr. Eric Clefstone. "Oh, Grimfield," he said cheerfully, looking up from his book. He had crinkles around his olive green eyes and a head of receding grey hair. Nate wondered why he bothered to continue dying his whiskers brown if he was letting his hair fall to the hands of time. "Go on, sit down," he motioned toward a chair, removing his glasses. "What do you need, son?"

"I've received a letter." He waved the paper in his hand, then inwardly cursed himself for stating the obvious. "It's from Bright Dawn Medical Treatment Center, in the States."

A strange expression came over Clefstone's face, "Well then," he reached out and Nate handed him the letter. He donned his glasses and read. The room was silent except for the ticking of the clock on the wall.

He set the letter down and looked up at Nate, removing his spectacles, "Good job, son. It's really something to catch the attention of the directors at Bright Dawn." He chuckled, "I was going to hire you on here full-time, but I wouldn't want you to pass up an opportunity like this. Guess we'll find some other chap to fill the slot." He stood and shook Nate's hand, "Good luck, son."

~~~~~~~~~~~~~~~~~~~~~~~~~~~

"Dr. Morris Richardson,

As a medical and psychiatric student, I have heard much about Bright Dawn and its reputation. I am thrilled to join your elite staff and hope to bring something new to the team at Bright Dawn.

Sincerely, Dr. Nate Grimfield"

~~~~~~~~~~~~~~~~~~~~~~~~~~~~

Nate descended the steps from the plane, the smell of the lake and the cold of November delightfully tickling his senses. He quickly found the car that Dr. Richardson had said would be waiting for him, obviously a company car. The license plate read "BRTDWN3." It was a black luxury sedan with taupe leather interior. He put his two suitcases and satchel in the trunk, then began the two hour drive from the airport to Pelf, the village that bordered Bright Dawn.

~~~~~~~~~~~~~~~~~~~~~~~~~~~~

Nate was relieved when he finally spotted a sign that read "Welcome to Pelf." It had been two hours of nothing but snow-covered hills and endless road, and he had found himself nodding off at the wheel. Because of the jetlag or bleak setting, he was not sure - maybe a mixture of both. A large black iron fence came into view, "B D" set in an arch over it. He drove between two large brick columns and down the long asphalt road. A large white building came into view, about six stories tall with grey windows and some floors that had small barred squares for windows. He swore he saw eyes watching him pull up through some of those bars. Nate pulled into a parking spot next to two large white vans; likely for transporting patients.

He got out of the car and grabbed his satchel out of the trunk, slinging it over his shoulder. He approached the glass double doors, so polished that they appeared blue. The lobby he entered was all white. A woman sat at a very neat central desk, laden only with a computer, a few papers, a phone, and a cup of pens. The woman wore an all-white dress suit with her long blonde hair in a ponytail, a few stray strands falling into her face.

"May I help you?" The woman asked in an airy voice. Nate did not hear her though; he was still taking in the facility. "May I help you?" she said louder, snapping him out of his daze.

"Yes, I'm Nate Grimfield. I'm supposed to meet with Dr. Richardson."

"Just a moment," she picked up the phone and dialed, then waited. "Yes... there's someone here to see you... Nate Grimfield...... thank you, Doctor," she hung up the phone and looked back at Nate. "He'll be down in a moment."

The elevator dinged and a tall man stepped out. He appeared to be middle-aged, his grey hair peppered with brown and accompanying well-groomed whiskers. He had light blue eyes framed by round wire glasses.

"Dr. Grimfield!" he said cheerfully, shaking Nate's hand. He had an accent Nate could not quite place. "We are very happy to have you here at Bright Dawn. How was your trip?"

"Long, but good. It's good to be here, sir."

"Well, come along, I have some things to show you. A sort of 'tour'; Bright Dawn is a large place. It was a state prison back in the 1800s, but got closed down in 1897. A man named Richard Dixon started it as a psychiatric hospital in 1922." He led Nate into the elevator. "He died only ten years after Bright Dawn was opened, but his legacy continued." The elevator stopped on the third floor. "I came here thirty years ago and became head doctor seven years after that.

"Most of the doctors here live onsite." They passed several rooms with small windows set in the doors: patients' rooms Nate assumed. Everything was white: the walls, the ceilings, the floors, the doors, the *clothes*.

"I am sorry to report that we do not have your quarters ready yet, but we have arranged for you to stay at the inn in Pelf until they are ready. So, patients are in the Central and North wings, the North being high security, doctors in the South, nurses in the East-" he realized Nate was no longer beside him. Nate was staring at a set of double doors, rusty blue with blacked out windows instead of clean white.

"What's in there?" Nate asked curiously.

"That's the West Wing," Dr. Richardson replied solemnly, "and it is off limits. It hasn't been renovated since Dixon opened the center, and it's not a safe place." His tone grew cheerful again, "So that's the third floor. The second floor is strictly medicine storage, therapy rooms, and guards' quarters. The fourth and fifth floors are for surgery and the sixth is where you can find my office. Doctors' offices are dispersed on the third floor, location based on patients. And the morgue and boiler room are in the basement - not that you need to go down there. Work begins at 8 A.M. sharp. Lunch at 12:30. Breaks when you see fit or no patients need your immediate care. Work ends promptly at 8 P.M. Lights out is roughly 10:30… not to say you can't work later if you feel the need.

"There are restrooms on every floor, but showers and washrooms are located on the first floor, as well as the kitchen, dining hall, and lounge. And that reminds me, breakfast is served at 6:30 A.M. and dinner at 8:30 P.M. There is also a small chapel located near the dining hall, off the courtyard, and we have one onsite cleric. Any questions, Dr. Grimfield?" He put his hands together as if in prayer and turned to Nate.

"No sir."

"Good, now I can show you some of the interesting stuff and then introduce you to your assistant nurse." He led Nate back to the elevator, and they stopped on the second floor. Dr. Richardson led him to a room labeled 'Music Therapy,' "Look," he said, motioning toward the window.

Nate looked. He saw a man with a shaved head in typical patient attire: white T-shirt, white pants, white slippers. He was playing a piano. He did not seem focused, looking blankly at the keys with round blue eyes.

"He plays the same few notes, every day, over and over again," Richardson said, and Nate put his ear to the door. The melody was

19

almost fast, but also sad, haunting, repeating, echoing in his mind. He quickly pulled his ear away.

"His name is William Redmoor. He suffers from a possible schizotypal disorder, making him a low functioning patient with a high suicide risk, but he has been officially diagnosed as having an unclassified mental illness." They both looked at him again. "I'm glad you got here when you did. He's scheduled to be the first to receive a new type of brain surgery. Two phases; he will be receiving Phase One tomorrow."

There was an awkward silence, and Nate looked up to see Richardson staring at William intensely. Nate looked at him a moment longer before Richardson came back to life. "Anyway, it's time to introduce you to your assistant nurse. Follow me." This time they took the stairs down to the first floor. Richardson led him to the lounge.

A young man was sitting there with short light blonde hair parted on the side, sticking out slightly in the back where it rested on his neck. He looked up, his hazel eyes shifting from Richardson to Nate, then stood and shook Nate's hand.

"This is Nigel Brauer, your assigned nursing assistant. Brauer, this is Dr. Nate Grimfield."

"Nice to meet you," Nigel nodded and smiled subtly.

"Well," Dr. Richardson clapped his hands together, "get acquainted, then feel free to explore, Grimfield. Just don't get lost. You'll get a list of patients tomorrow." He walked away, leaving the two young men in silence.

"So you're from London?" Nigel asked.

"Yes, born and raised there. You?"

"Kansas."

They were silent again. "What do you know about patient William Redmoor?"

Nigel's eyes widened and he frowned uncomfortably. "He murdered his wife and daughter. The photos were terrible… cut them into little pieces, with-" he stopped. "He's an extreme case. Psycho as they come. But they're operating on him tomorrow."

"Yes, I know. Dr. Richardson mentioned it."

"I see." Nigel stood. "I'm going to make some coffee. Want some?"

"No thanks, think I'll go have a look around."

Chapter 2

Nate stepped out into the snow once more. He was about to climb into the car when someone shouted, "Hey! What do you think you're doing?" He turned to see a man in a navy uniform sporting a silver badge, a night stick, and a pistol holstered to his waist.

"Going into Pelf!" he shouted back. "I'm staying at the inn there!"

The man laughed; he had a booming laugh, "They don't drive cars in Pelf! No roads!" He lumbered over to where Nate stood. As he approached, Nate could see he had uncombed auburn hair and dark eyes and was a pretty sizable man; not fat, but muscular and tall. "Reese Caulderstone, head of security," he shook Nate's hand.

"Nate Grimfield. I'm a new doctor here."

"So *you're* the new kid. I can drive you over to the village limits, but I can't drive inside it."

"Thank you." Nate handed him the keys and climbed into the car. The ride was short, maybe five minutes. Nate got the idea Reese had only offered to drive him to chew his ear. He was still going on about what he had seen some nurse doing when Nate climbed out of the car, thanked him - which went unnoticed - and retrieved his things from the trunk. He observed that the entrance to Pelf was a large wooden gate, which was currently open. As a matter of fact, the whole place seemed to be contained inside kind of a fort, with barbed wire coiled around the top of the walls. All of the buildings were made of logs with stone foundations. It looked as if they had been built back in the early 1800s.

He spotted a building with a sign that read 'Mosher's General Store.' A somewhat heavyset man with shaggy reddish-blonde hair and a thick beard and mustache walked out the doors as he passed. He waved when he noticed Nate. Nate reluctantly changed his course and approached the man.

"You're new here, aren't you?" His olive-green eyes met Nate's blue. "Owen Rice," he offered his hand, "new caretaker of the lighthouse, only been here about two weeks."

"Dr. Nate Grimfield, newly employed at the Bright Dawn Treatment Center. Could you show me the way to the inn?"

"It's just down the road; you can't miss it," he pointed. "Well, it's not a road, but the 'path.' You'll learn soon enough that to get lost in Pelf, you have to try." They began down the path, passing a large central fountain. "So where're you from? I was the operator of a lighthouse in Rhode Island until they had it condemned. I'd grown to love the place," he looked down sadly. "They no longer operate the lighthouse here; but it's kind of iconic, and they wanted someone to take care of it."

"I'm from London," Nate replied. "I just finished medical school and a doctor internship when Bright Dawn found me."

"I hear Bright Dawn used to be a prison. But the people around here haven't been willing to tell me more about it. They still view me as an outsider. A few have been friendly though, like Vincent Hoover the innkeeper, even though he is a little excitable. I guess not having many guests and being so close to the hospital has gone to his nerves. And the Pratchett brothers aren't too bad... perhaps a little too friendly."

Nate spotted a three-story building with a sign that read 'Great Lake Inn.' It was like all of the other buildings, built of logs with a stone foundation. "What *do* you know about Bright Dawn?" Nate asked, his eyes drawn to the third floor of the inn.

"The obvious. Just that it's a medical treatment center for mentally unstable people, and I already told you that I heard it used to be a prison." They stopped under the awning of the inn. "Well, here we are," Owen offered his hand once more, "Welcome to Pelf." Nate shook his hand, and then entered the inn.

"Oh! You must be Nate Grimfield!" Nate saw a man coming from behind the counter. He had a slender, feminine face framed by mutton chops; to make him appear more masculine, Nate guessed. He had a crew-cut, and what little hair he had appeared to be light brown. His blue eyes remained locked on Nate as he wiped his hands on his apron. "Your room is ready, I'll take you up?" he offered; Nate noticed his whole body was trembling.

"Sure."

"I'm Vincent Hoover by the way," he said, leading Nate to the second floor. "You are the only one staying here at the present time, so you won't have to worry about other guests disturbing you." He unlocked a door and opened it for Nate. "You're in Room 202." He handed Nate the key. "We'll bring dinner up to you in about an hour?"

"That should be fine. I may be out for a bit trying to learn my way around."

"Oh, yes, of course," he smiled, a little too big. Nate noticed he was wringing his hands. His smile shrank, "There isn't much to see, however." He backed out of the room, then turned and hurried back down the stairs.

"Owen was right," Nate said to himself, "a *little* excitable." He chuckled at his own sarcasm.

He set his bags down by the bed and looked around the room. It was not much: just a bed, chair, desk, and bathroom, with a small closet set off to the side. He pulled a coat out of one of his bags and put it on before going back out into the cold.

When he stepped out of the inn, he decided to head to the docks first. The lake was beautiful, frozen and lightly dusted with snow. He noticed a building with a red sign that read 'Pratchett Bros Imports & Exports.' He approached and entered the building. It looked like a storage warehouse filled with all kinds of junk. A young man came from the back room, hauling a box. He had short dark brown hair combed back neatly, matching stubble, and friendly blue eyes.

"Hi, can I help you?" He set down the box he was carrying with a thud. "You must be new here... I don't recognize you. Bill Pratchett," he extended his hand to Nate.

"Nate Grimfield. Yes, you're right about me being new-"

"Accent gave you away." Another young man came from the back room with blonde instead of brown hair styled the same way. Nate noticed he also had the same blue eyes, but was more clean-shaven. "And let me guess, Bright Dawn? I'd heard rumors they were hiring someone new up there. Biff Pratchett, by the way." He shook Nate's hand.

"So you two own this?" Nate asked, pointing at another 'Pratchett Bros' sign hanging on the wall.

"Nope," Bill replied.

"Dad does," Biff added.

"He had a brother."

"But they weren't twins."

"Grandpa started the business, named it after his sons."

"The Y-chromosome runs deep in our family," Biff laughed. "So what can I do ya for, Dr. Grimfield?"

"Well, you can just call me Nate," he smiled, "and I'm basically trying to learn my way around Pelf." He paused. "I heard Bright Dawn used to be a state prison?"

"Yeah… a long time ago," Bill replied.

"Any reason it's not a prison now?"

"Because now it's Bright Dawn?" Biff said. "About Pelf," he cleared his throat, "Greg Mosher, the general store owner, is an asshole."

"Biff!"

"Well it's true."

"You know Dad would kill you if he heard you talking like that at work," Bill exclaimed.

"Not like he's ever here…"

Nate looked quizzically at Bill.

"Dad may own the business," Bill answered Nate's silent question, "but we run it."

"Dad quit coming around here when Uncle Cliff left."

"Yeah-" the door opened and a young woman walked in. She had long straight black hair and light brown eyes.

"Katie!" Biff called out, "You look wonderful this evening!"

"How can I help you this evening, Katie?" Bill asked, smiling charmingly at her.

"I was actually looking for Dr. Grimfield." She turned to him, "Vincent doesn't want your dinner to get cold."

"Oh, yes, it would just *kill* Vincent Hoover for his only customer ever to be unhappy," Biff laughed mockingly.

"Just Nate is fine," he took her hand, "Katie…?"

"Katie Mackle. I work at the inn with Vincent. I do the things he can't do… like cook."

"Well, I guess I'll get going so that dinner doesn't get cold." He turned to the twins. "It was nice meeting you."

"Same." Bill smiled, then shifted back to Katie, "Bye, Katie."

"Bye, Bill," she whispered. She looked toward Biff, who was heading for the back room, "Bye, Biff!"

He didn't answer.

"It's obvious we're twins," Nate barely heard Bill say to himself as he followed Katie back out into the chilly evening.

~~~~~~~~~~~~~~~~~~~~~~~~~~

Nate pulled up the collar of his coat as he walked out into the brisk morning. Snow was falling down slowly, making the whole place seem so quaint. He looked off toward the sunrise and thought of William Redmoor's surgery scheduled for today. Perhaps this could be a new beginning for this man who had killed his wife and child out of insanity; the dawn of a new life.

Before he walked out of Pelf's gates, he stepped into Mosher's General Store. Inside it was warm, but there was a musty smell. Everything appeared to be covered in a light coat of dust. Apparently Mosher's did not sell products at a very fast rate.

He noticed a man sitting in a chair behind what appeared to be the front counter. He was a thick man, appearing to be in the decline of his middle-aged years. He had gruff brows which covered brown eyes, and whiskers that just covered the lower half of his face. His short scruffy hair looked as though he had attempted to part it, ending in failure, a disheveled greying brown.

"Can I 'elp you with somethin'?" he growled.

"I was just looking around." Nate suddenly forgot why he had walked into the general store. "I'm Nate Grimfield, I work at Bright Dawn," he extended his hand.

The owner glared up at him, "Greg Mosher… You gonna buy anything?"

Nate withdrew his hand, "I heard the center used to be a state prison, what do you know about that?"

"Look, either buy somethin' or get the 'ell outta my shop! I don't much care for chitchat."

Nate stood in silence for a moment, then slowly turned from him. "I'm sorry for bothering you."

He exited the gate and made his way down the road to Bright Dawn. The walk was not long; he was now sure that Reese had driven him the day before just to chew his ear.

He walked through the doors and once again was greeted by the receptionist, whose name he had found out was Mary Alexander. She was cute; he had not realized how beautifully shaped her nose was yesterday. She also smiled at him today, only adding to her cuteness in Nate's opinion.

He rode the elevator to the third floor and wandered from office to office until he found one with a blank upper label and the one beneath reading 'Brauer, N.' He walked in to find Nigel drinking coffee and organizing his desk.

"You look cold," Nigel commented, looking up. "Red nose and ears. You won't have to make the chilly hike once they have your room fixed."

"Fixed?"

"The heating's out. And apparently the doctor who stayed there prior spilled some patient's blood work all over the carpet, so that needs to be replaced as well."

"Interesting." Nate hung his coat on an empty rack by the door. "When is Redmoor's surgery scheduled?"

"Ten, so we've got about two hours. Richardson wanted you in his office when you arrived. Sixth floor, remember?"

"Yes, thank you." He pulled on a white lab coat that had been draped over the back of his chair with 'Grimfield' embroidered on the right breast pocket.

When he arrived on the sixth floor, he was shocked to see everything was not white and shades of blue. It was all dark wood paneling, accented by deep red wallpaper. The lights were dim and the carpet was a dark - almost black - green. A miniature ivory plaque that read 'Dr. Morris P. Richardson' hung on the wall outside of an ebony door with a brass knob.

He knocked. He could hear classical music playing on the other side of the door - Beethoven he thought. He heard a click, and the music ceased.

"Yes, who is it?"

"Nate Grimfield."

"Oh, good... yes, come in Grimfield."

He entered to see the same colors as in the hall, with a hardwood floor and the same black-green shag rugs.

"You wanted to see me?"

"Yes, about your new patients. There is a list, with short biographies and their treatments; I will give you that in a moment. And I assure you, I didn't start you out with high security patients." He smiled, "You'll be at Redmoor's surgery this morning, Grimfield?"

"Yes sir."

"Good." He clapped his hands together enthusiastically. "You'll be observing history in the making, my boy! Now where did I put that damned clipboard... ah yes!" He took a clipboard from his desk and gave it to Nate. "Your patients. Get acquainted... but don't be

31

late." He winked, "If you need anything, just come up, and I will assist you as best I can. Brauer has a good head on his shoulders too."

"Yes, I'm sure Nigel will be a great help." Nate took the clipboard and left Richardson's office.

He entered his and Nigel's office and began to go through his list of patients. He had six; Richardson had left a note that they preferred each doctor to have as few patients as possible so they could pay special attention to each individual.

His first patient was named Wallace Dodson (and/or Michael Pierre), a man suffering from multiple personality disorder.

Next came Alice Pink, who suffered from severe paranoia. At the young age of sixteen, she'd had a nervous breakdown, believing that 'they' were out to get her.

Jim Beam believed he lived in another world and was somewhat content to stay in it. He was completely out of touch with reality.

Jacob Richards, a suicidal maniac, was the only patient of his kept in a padded room and straight jacket, but he was not considered high security since he was only a danger to himself.

Milfred Barv, a woman suffering from Alzheimer's; all Nate could really do was keep her comfortable and happy.

Lastly, he came to Rodney Leach, who had murdered his sister because he said she was possessed by the Devil. He knew every verse of the Bible, frequently spewing verse after verse to doctors, guards, and patients. His lawyer had pled insanity; Nate could see why…

He flipped the page over and noticed a strange symbol carved into the wooden clipboard. As he leaned in to examine it, he noticed an arrow drawn lightly in black pen and written next to it, 'What is William trying to say?'

"Hey," Nate jumped as Nigel tapped his shoulder, "Sorry, but we need to get going, Redmoor's surgery starts in ten minutes and it's best if we're early."

"All right," Nate glanced at the symbol one last time before letting the papers cover it once more and following Nigel out of the room.

They rode up to the fourth floor and entered the observation area for Operation Room E. A young man sat in a chair inside and stood when they entered. "Nigel," he said cheerfully. He had short brown hair with a cowlick at the back, causing his hair to stick up. He had a mustache that rested just above his lip and green eyes framed by black thick-rimmed glasses.

"Nate, this is Keith McDonnell, my previous supervisor. Keith, Nate Grimfield."

"Nice to meet you, Nate," Keith shook his hand, "From London, right?"

"Yes. And yourself?"

"Wisconsin. You hear about Redmoor? What he did, I mean," Keith said as they wheeled the sedated Redmoor into the operating room. "He killed his wife and daughter… he never did say why. He was silent when they cross-examined him in court. Never spoke to his lawyer even, I heard. Guess there isn't much to say when you slaughter your wife and kid." He looked through the glass and sadly shook his head, "I don't see how anyone could do that to another living creature. He just-"

"Let's change the subject," Nate turned to see Nigel sweating profusely; he looked as though he was going to be sick. He dabbed his forehead with a handkerchief. "Besides, I think Richardson is about to begin." He pulled a chair up to the window.

Nate watched as a tall surgeon led three others into the operating room. They all wore white, with light blue gloves and face masks, and silver rimmed goggles with crystal clear lenses. He saw Richardson's blue eyes shoot up to the window for a moment and saw them light up when he spotted Nate.

Richardson's voice came over the speaker in the observatory, probably from a mic in his mask. "As of 10 A.M., William Redmoor has begun Phase One of the operation. Electric bone saw," he turned to the assistant on his right and took a small saw from him. He began to slowly sever Redmoor's skull cap nearly completely from his head.

"We can now see the complete top portion of Redmoor's brain, which from the outside would appear perfectly healthy. Scalpel," he leaned in and gently placed his left index finger and thumb around the area he was about to cut. Suddenly he cried out, pulling his hand back and shaking it as if he had been burned. The scalpel clattered to the floor.

One assistant rushed to him, looking at his hand and said something the observers could not hear.

"Yes, I'm fine," Richardson said, breathing fast through his mouth. "I'm sure it was just a static shock… new scalpel?" An assistant handed him an uncontaminated scalpel. "We shall now proceed." He bent and cut into Redmoor's brain.

~~~~~~~~~~~~~~~~~~~~~~~~~

After a time, Nigel left to use the restroom. Once he was out of the room, Keith looked over his shoulder, then leaned in to Nate. "He killed them with his bare hands. He ripped them up pretty good," his voice was a hushed whisper. "They found him covered in their blood and traces of skin under his nails." He shifted, "Nigel puked when he saw the pictures. He hates the subject. Some people do crazy things..." He looked back out the window as Nigel reappeared.

Other doctors and nurses came and went, including Keith who went to check on his patients. He returned with his current nursing assistant, an African American woman named Abigail Norris, who had black hair pulled back in a bun and brown eyes. She did not stay long however. She could not take seeing Richardson covered in so much blood. "It's not becoming to his good nature," she had said.

~~~~~~~~~~~~~~~~~~~~~~~~~

Richardson stood and his voice came through the speakers once more, "Surgery complete, as of 1:45 P.M. Replacing skull cap."

They put the cap back in place and began to stitch him up. Once he was sewn up, Richardson spoke again, "Checking vitals... heart rate: steady... breathing: slightly labored... brain activity: slightly below average, but he does not appear to be a vegetable... looks like he may be in a coma." There was a long silence, then, "Let the record show, that as of 3:33 P.M., the patient has survived Phase One of the operation. Prepare for Phase Two." The blood-splattered Richardson looked up at the window and the look in his eyes sent a chill down Nate's spine. He was glad he could not see the rest of the Doctor's expression.

He turned to see Nigel was gone, then inwardly cursed himself for getting so wrapped up in the operation. He had missed lunch and neglected his patients by not checking on them. He walked to the office and saw Nigel arranging files in a drawer.

"I checked up on the patients. Milfred asked if you were her husband's friend… and Rod said 'God Bless Him.'"

"I see," Nate took the clipboard from his desk. "I'll go meet them now."

Chapter 3

Nate sat in his room, the meatloaf and boiled potatoes on his plate growing cold as he stared at the symbol William had supposedly carved into the clipboard. It had three distinct parts, one semi-centered and the other two branching off jaggedly from it. Each of the three branches ended in a crooked polygon, with line drawings inside so small that Nate could not make them out. He took a sip of his apple cider and looked at the clock by his bed. It was after nine, he needed to rest for his work day tomorrow. He could hear jazz music coming through the floor from below him. Probably Vincent since there were no other guests. He ate most of his dinner, then lay down and quickly fell asleep.

He dreamed of his patients. Wallace, a man in his thirties with hazel eyes and a clean-shaven baby face had greeted him warmly, telling him about his new idea for a game design. Alice, a teen with short red hair and brown eyes had refused to speak to him because 'they' might overhear them. Jim, an older man with a blonde ponytail and stubble, seemed to have no idea who he or Nate was. Jacob, a man in his twenties with black hair and grey eyes, had remained curled up in his corner, asking Nate if he could see his pen, and Nate had politely declined. Rodney, a brown-haired dark brown-eyed middle-aged man, had recited Psalm 23:1, "The Lord is my shepherd, I shall not want." And he dreamed of Richardson's expression after the operation and the red blood on his white smock.

Nate awoke to a knock on his door, accompanied by the smell of pancakes and smoked bacon.

"Just a moment," he called as he climbed out into the cold from under his warm covers. He stepped down to find only one slipper; the other was lost under the bed. He finally located it and made his way to the door. There stood Katie with a tray covered in pancakes, bacon, butter, and hot chocolate.

"Good morning, Dr. Grimfield."

"Nate. Good morning, Katie," he opened the door wider and motioned with his arm, "Would you like to come in?"

"Sure," she smiled and brought the tray in, setting it on his desk.

"Who all comes through Pelf?"

"Not very many people, it's just kind of out of the way. Mostly doctors' families and the few people who aren't completely ashamed of their committed relatives. And the occasional salesman; the Pratchett brothers do make some business deals. They're the biggest thing going on in Pelf besides Bright Dawn." She paused a moment as Nate took his first bite of bacon. "How is it?"

"Delicious," he smiled.

"What about London? What was that like?"

"Much busier than here... cars and roads everywhere, lots of people. I do kind of miss it." He stared out the window. "But it's much more beautiful here." He smiled again, almost sadly, his gaze distant.

"It's always snowy here," she joined him by the window. "I'd like to see London someday... or Paris maybe."

"Perhaps you will. You're still young; you have a lot of time ahead of you."

She giggled. "You're not too old yourself, Nate Grimfield." She looked out the window, "I've got to get going... it was nice talking to you, Nate."

"Same with you, Katie." As she left, he turned back to the window. He noticed a tall dark figure making his way through the snow, and as he got closer, Nate recognized him as Bill Pratchett. Katie appeared, trotting toward him; and they embraced, then took each other's hands and began walking toward the docks, talking intently.

He smiled to himself as he thought of Mary. His smile shrank when he thought of Biff Pratchett. It had been made quite clear the other day that he loved Katie too, but he just was not the one she had chosen. Nate had been an only child, so he could only imagine the heartbreak of watching the one you love be with your brother, whom you also love. He sat down to finish his pancakes; he did not have much longer until he had to be at Bright Dawn.

~~~~~~~~~~~~~~~~~~~~~~~~~~

Nate sat down in the mess hall to eat his sandwich, which appeared to be ham and some other mystery meat. When he was finished, he walked outside into the snowy courtyard, breathing in the fresh air. Another door opened and an elderly man dressed all in black stepped out, leaving his foot in the door. He was average-height, with receding grey hair and blue eyes. He motioned at Nate.

"Hey, are you Dr. Grimfield?" He had a very slight Irish accent.

"Yes." Nate put his hands in his pockets as the old man motioned for him to follow.

"Come in, I want to talk to you." Nate slowly approached the man and when he was close enough, he extended his hand. "I'm Chaplain Kennedy. How much time can you spare?"

Nate checked his watch, "Well, I need to be back in my office in about twenty minutes."

Once inside, the Chaplain led him through what appeared to be the interior of a small church.

"It's for when a patient dies... not like many people show up. No one is willing to claim the poor cretins. Grimfield, you're new - do you mind if I call you Nate?" Nate shook his head. "Good, well, Nate, you're new here, so I'm wondering if you have noticed that there is something not quite right here at Bright Dawn... a secret."

"Secret? What kind of secret?" Nate was suddenly painfully interested, thinking of the guarded villagers.

"I don't have time to go into it now," he looked around and whispered, "just watch your back."

"But-"

"I've seen this place swallow people whole and I don't want to see that happen to you," he shook his head sadly. "They start so young... Come see me later, I'll tell you more... You know any of the guards?"

"No, well, aside from Reese Caulderstone."

"There's not a soul here who doesn't know *him*. But I'd suggest getting to know Dean Miller. Sometimes it's good to not talk only to the doctors and Dean's a good man... smart." He motioned to a small room at the back of the church. "You can find me in my office. Good to meet you, Nate." He shook his hand, "I hope you can help these people here at Bright Dawn."

"I'll do my best," Nate said, wondering about the secret and who this 'Dean Miller' was.

~~~~~~~~~~~~~~~~~~~~~~~~~~~

The corridors were empty; everyone was either in their offices or with their patients. Nate slowly approached the dirty blue rusted doors. He looked both ways before pulling on the handle. The door shifted, but did not open. He pushed, and still the door remained closed. It appeared to be locked from the inside, which did not make sense if no one had been *in* there for years.

He turned and began to walk away when something pushed the door from the other side, hard. He fell backwards, shouting. His cry was answered by a beastly roar and another vicious jolt to the door...

Nate jerked awake to see the janitor, who Nigel referred to as Slim, opening the door to the office. He looked surprised when he saw Nate slumped over his desk.

"I thought you'd be gone, Dr. Grimfield."

Nate glanced at a clock and saw it was past midnight. He wiped his face and ran his hand through his hair before standing and pulling on his coat. "I must've fallen asleep," he slung his satchel over his shoulder. "Good night, Slim."

"'Night sir."

As Nate walked through the dimly lit halls, he passed the doors to the West Wing. He stopped, trying to squint through their blacked out windows, but decades of stain made it impossible to see anything. He brushed the handle with his hand and laughed at himself for thinking there was anyone behind the doors. As he walked away, he did not notice the fluorescent bulb over the doors begin to flicker.

~~~~~~~~~~~~~~~~~~~~~~~~~~~

At 6:30 A.M., Nate made his way down to the lobby of the inn. He turned when a blast of cold air hit him from the left and he saw Bill looking around, his typically well-groomed hair falling into his eyes. He spotted Nate and approached him.

"Have you seen Katie this morning?"

"She knocked on my door around five, which is when I requested breakfast this morning, but she left it outside. Sorry."

"Eh, it's fine." He looked down at an envelope he had in his hands and flipped it over several times between his fingers before looking back up at Nate. "I don't trust Hoover; when you see her, will you give her this for me?" He offered the envelope to Nate.

"Why do you trust me? I've only been here for about a week."

"Because she does." He looked pleadingly at Nate.

Nate took the envelope. "I'll do it."

"Thank you," and Bill was gone as quickly as he had appeared.

Nate looked around and spotted Vincent Hoover cleaning behind the counter. "Excuse me," he leaned in, and Hoover looked up at him. "Do you happen to know where Katie is?"

"She went into town for some groceries, can't say when she'll be back… I can help you if you need anything."

"No, it's fine, I just need to tell her something, that's all." Nate turned and walked out the door, and made his way to Bright Dawn.

He dropped his satchel off in his office, went down to the church, and found Chaplain Kennedy in his office.

"Hello, Chaplain."

"Nate!" He seemed both surprised and pleased to see him. "You kept your word, you came back."

"Yes… I have noticed things about Bright Dawn. And Pelf. Like the guarded villagers."

"Yes, they do tend to be that way. I myself was born and raised in Pelf. My father was the preacher there."

"Then you know about the prison?"

"Yes."

Nate leaned in, so eager he was rhythmically tapping his foot. "Why did it close down?" His voice was a hoarse whisper.

"I will show you." Chaplain Kennedy went to a file cabinet and pulled out a yellowed newspaper. The headline read 'Prisoner Riot Closes Down Pelf State Prison.' According to the article, a dense fog bank had covered the exercise yard, leaving dead guards and prisoners in its wake. The surviving tower guards later described sounds they had heard coming from below as 'unmistakably beastly.'

Nate looked up, wide-eyed, "So it was just a prisoner riot?"

"That's what they reported. The tower guards couldn't see anything because of the fog and no one below lived to tell what had happened. Supposedly some of them are buried in the exercise yard. But we don't have access there."

"Where is that?"

"Through the West Wing."

Nate felt a lump growing in his throat, and he thought of his dream; the terrible roar he had heard behind the door. He shook his head, laughing at himself. It was just his imagination and curiosity getting the better of him.

"But that wasn't the only inciden-"

"Dr. Nate Grimfield." Richardson's voice came over the intercom. "Dr. Nate Grimfield, please report to Dr. Richardson's office at once. Thank you."

Nate looked at the Chaplain in disappointment.

"There will be many more times for that story, Nate. For now, go to Richardson." He returned the newspaper to his file cabinet.

As he rode the elevator, Nate suddenly felt uneasy. He shrugged the feeling off, that article and the talk with the Chaplain had just gotten him worked up. The elevator dinged and he stepped off. This time he could hear Bach through Richardson's door.

He knocked. "Just a moment, Grimfield." The music went off and Richardson came to the door and opened it. "I have good news for you!" His smile seemed almost forced. "They should have your room ready after the weekend. Why don't you take the weekend off to get prepared, and you can resume work on Monday when you move in?"

"All right," Nate turned to leave when Richardson put his hand on his shoulder, which was so cold that Nate could feel it through his clothes. Nate turned back to him.

"Have you seen any of the high security cases?" he hissed in Nate's ear.

"No, I haven't, sir," Nate suddenly realized how pale the Doctor looked.

"Bizarre and intriguing… you should look into that when you get the chance. North Wing." He patted Nate's shoulder, "I'm glad you're with us, Nate."

Nate nodded uncomfortably, and then took the elevator down to the third floor. As he got off, he noticed something flickering and looked around. His gaze stopped on the fluorescent bulb over the doors to the West Wing. It was flickering, causing both an annoying strobe light effect and a buzzing sound. He made a mental note to tell Slim later. He grabbed his clipboard and began making his rounds.

When he reached Rodney's room, he opened the door and walked in. "Good morning, Rodney."

"Good morning, sir, it's a lovely morning-" he stopped short when he looked at Nate, his eyes widening. He slowly raised his hand to point at him; his whole arm was shaking, "Evil has touched you," he whispered and began to shake more violently. "You're unclean!" He suddenly began to shout, "Out, demon, *out!*" He shoved Nate against the wall, then rigorously wiped his hands on his pants before retreating to a far corner and putting his hands over his ears and screaming at the top of his lungs.

45

Nate just sat and stared at him, breathing hard, when Keith McDonnell suddenly burst through the door, looking first at Nate, then at Rodney.

"Would you please stop screaming, Rodney? You're disturbing the others," Keith said in an even, but slightly pleading tone.

Rodney looked up at Keith, his face covered in perspiration and his teeth gritted. "He has been touched by the Devil," he pointed at Nate, "get him out!"

Keith helped Nate up and guided him out the door, saying, "He's leaving," over his shoulder to Rodney, pulling the door closed behind them.

Nate leaned on the water cooler, and Keith poured him a cup of water. "That was new," Keith said after a moment of silence, "all he's done since he got here is spew Bible verses… you all right?"

"Yeah," Nate replied, taking another big swig of water.

"What'd you do to provoke him?"

"Nothing," Nate coughed, "I just said 'good morning.'"

Keith stroked his mustache, frowning pensively. "That's odd… well as long as you're okay."

Nate nodded. Keith gave the thumbs up and smiled. It was then that Nate noticed the gold band on his left ring finger.

~~~~~~~~~~~~~~~~~~~~~~~~~~

Nate was folding the last of his shirts when a knock came at his door. "Come in." It was Katie with dinner. He blushed, realizing he must look like a mess with his tie loosened, his top two buttons undone, and his shirt untucked.

"Meatloaf again."

"It was good the first time."

"Thanks... you're leaving?" she looked past him at the packed suitcases and now- empty closet.

"Yes. They'll have my room ready at Bright Dawn by Monday."

"I'll miss you," she said, her eyes sad even though she was smiling. "It gets lonely here... it's been nice having someone to talk to."

"You know the Pratchett brothers," he said, then suddenly ran over to his dresser. "Speaking of which, Bill told me to give you this." He took the envelope from his satchel.

She took it from him. "Thank you... well I'll leave you to your dinner."

~~~~~~~~~~~~~~~~~~~~~~~~~~~~

Nate crested the last step to the top of the lighthouse and was surrounded by the morning light. The view was amazing, overlooking the frozen lake and snowy landscape on all sides. Owen Rice stood by one of the windows, polishing it with an old shirt. Nate flipped up the collar of his coat; they say heat rises, but he did not feel the least bit warm at the top of this tower.

"Beautiful morning," Nate said, approaching Owen; he could see his breath as he spoke.

Owen looked up, "Why, Nate Grimfield! Good morning, Doctor, yes, very lovely morning." He shook Nate's hand firmly, "So how've you been?"

"Good, this Bright Dawn thing really seems to be working out. What about you? Feeling any more welcome in Pelf?"

"Eh, sort of. I'm still the outsider, just like you Doctor. But those Pratchett brothers," he shook his head, chuckling. "They're quite the pair. Nice boys, nice boys..."

"Yes, this is the kind of place that seems like it hasn't changed in decades. Walking into Pelf is like walking into an old movie," Nate looked out over the log and stone village. "Katie Mackle has been friendly, have you met her?"

"The young girl at the inn? I've only seen her once or twice, but she had a nice walk... not the stooped creep of the other villagers." He went over the window one last time with the shirt. "I did find out this used to be a coal mining village, back in the 1940s. I even found an old mine shaft not too far from the lighthouse." He pointed out the window. "I'm thinking I might explore that later, I bought a headlamp from that codger Mosher yesterday."

"Interesting."

"So I hear you're leaving Pelf soon." Owen turned back to Nate. Totally blind-sided, Nate stuttered when he replied,

"W-word travels fast around here."

Owen laughed, a gravelly sound, "Biff Pratchett told me. Good luck, Nate."

"Thank you," Nate shook his hand and turned to leave, but stopped. "There was one more thing... I heard Chaplain Kennedy, up at the hospital's father used to be the minister here. Who preaches here now?"

Owen shifted uncomfortably. "Nobody does." He seemed to have the same guarded tone as the villagers for a moment, but it faded away. "I wouldn't bring him up here, the villagers all feel like he abandoned them for the money of hospital cleric after his father died. No one goes to the church here anymore... or the cemetery."

"Well if no one goes to the cemetery, who's buried there? Someone must go out there to bury people."

"Coal miners. The cemetery is *under*ground."

Nate felt a knot forming where his heart should be; he suddenly thought of the inmates buried in the exercise yard. "I see."

Owen nodded slowly, then smiled warmly at Nate, "But enough about that, I'm sure you have places to be and things to do, Doctor. Good-bye, and good luck."

"I'm sure I'll see you when I stop into Pelf every now and then."

Owen smiled uncertainly, "If you come by. You'll get busy. Doctors are seldom seen in Pelf."

~~~~~~~~~~~~~~~~~~~~~~~~~~~

Nate slung his satchel over his shoulder and was going to lift his two suitcases when Katie walked in - he had left the door open.

"You're leaving."

"Yes, it's Monday morning."

"Can I help you with your things?"

"You don't need to do that."

"Vincent will have a cow if I don't," she stifled a laugh.

Nate could not argue, so he just let her take the lighter suitcase. They descended the stairs to find Vincent wringing his hands and smiling too big.

"How was your stay, Dr. Grimfield? I hope you found everything satisfactory." He was quivering; he reminded Nate of a small dog.

"Yes, Mr. Hoover, everything has been wonderful."

Vincent beamed with pride, and then retreated behind the counter; probably to attend to some sweeping and jazz music.

The two stepped out into the cold. "You don't have to carry that all the way to the gate," Nate said.

"I can manage."

"Katie!" Biff Pratchett's voice rang out and he waved from a distance, then began jogging over.

Nate persisted, "Really, it's fine, you're not even wearing a coat-"

"Let me get that," Biff arrived, relieving Katie of the suitcase and not noticing the hurt look on her face. "Good morning, Nate. Cold morning."

"Biff, I've got it," Katie tried to take the suitcase back.

"You need to get back inside where it's warm." He suddenly grew serious, his eyes meeting hers. "It's below freezing today; you really shouldn't be out without a coat." He rubbed her arm.

She was suddenly fighting tears, "You're right, he's no longer *my* customer. Good-bye, Nate." She turned slowly and went inside.

Biff stared after her a moment before turning back to Nate and saying, "It's not often people leave Pelf. Nobody comes in to go out… and the doctors never stay here, their quarters are *always* ready when they arrive." They began toward the gate. "Please tell me you don't have to lug this all the way to Bright Dawn?"

"No, they're sending over a car," Nate laughed.

The morning was still and quiet, so they both looked up as Greg Mosher emerged from his shop. Biff was suddenly flushed. "Pardon me; I just remembered Bill needs help with some boxes at the docks. Cheerio, Nate," he added a terribly fake accent to his 'Cheerio' and set the briefcase down before taking off. Nate picked it up and continued toward the gate.

"'ey. 'ey!" Nate ignored Mosher's yelling; it was not the first time he had heard the man carry on during his short time in Pelf. "'ey! Get back here, you bloody bastard!"

Nate stopped and whipped around, insulted. Mosher continued toward him, out of breath. He stopped, bending over and supporting his upper body weight by resting his hand on his knee. He was breathing heavily through his mouth.

"Owe… Owen Rice," he was attempting to speak between breaths and his gravelly voice made him nearly impossible to understand, "told… told me t-… to give you… this," he extended his hand. He held a small key attached to a nautical keychain with a small anchor on it.

"When did he give you this?" Nate frowned curiously.

"This mornin'… he was in one hell of a 'urry. Looked all riled up and was carrying some kinda box," he frowned at Nate. "Jus' take the damn key so I can get back in outta the cold!"

Nate took the key and Mosher headed back to his shop, cussing under his breath. "Quite an unpleasant fellow," Nate said to himself before heading out the gate to the white van that awaited him. He was greeted by a husky man in a denim ball cap. He silently rejoiced in the fact that it was not Reese Caulderstone.

"Sorry I've gotta pick you up like this," the driver said apologetically, "but I don't have clearance to use the company cars."

"It's all right," Nate said, although on the short ride to Bright Dawn, he could not help feeling like an inmate being shipped in.

Chapter 4

Nigel met Nate as the van pulled up to Bright Dawn. Nate's spirits were dampened when he noticed that Nigel did not look happy.

He climbed out of the van. "Good morning, Nate," Nigel's voice was no more enthusiastic than his expression. He looked to make sure the driver was out of earshot. "Caulderstone has to go through all your things as a 'security check.' Pretty soon the whole facility will know what brand of underwear you wear." Now Nate knew why Nigel looked glum.

"I'll survive, it's a British brand anyway," he joked, trying to brighten the mood of the cold morning.

"Yeah," Nigel smiled slightly. "I'll show you to your room?"

They rode the elevator to the third floor, then Nigel led Nate to the South Wing, where all the doctors stayed. As they passed the entrance to the West Wing, Nate noticed the faulty bulb had been changed.

His room was about midway down the South corridor. Reese Caulderstone stood just inside the door. "I'll only take a moment." Reese began to go through Nate's things and Nigel coughed. Reese did not seem to find anything that interested him, and quickly excused himself.

"I'll see you in the office, ten minutes," Nate said and Nigel nodded in understanding. Once he was gone, Nate closed the door and retrieved the key from his pocket. Scribbled on the back of the keychain in what appeared to be Sharpie marker was the word 'spare.'

Nate put it on the desk, deciding to ask Owen about it the next time he was in Pelf.

He looked around the room. The walls were painted a dark blue, the bed against the West and South walls, a desk against the North with a leather rolling chair, a closet right next to the desk, and a dresser next to the door. A small cabinet sat by the bed with a small digital clock and a lamp setting upon it. He put his suitcases in the closet and his satchel on the bed before heading for the office.

~~~~~~~~~~~~~~~~~~~~~~~~

The sky was dark, almost black, strange puffy green clouds blocking out any real blue sky. Nate could suddenly hear screams…

He sat straight up in bed, covered in sweat even though his room could not have been more than sixty-five degrees. He could feel his heart pounding in his chest.

"Just a dream," he said after a few moments and lay back down, hoping to get back to sleep.

~~~~~~~~~~~~~~~~~~~~~~~~

Redmoor's surgery had been a week and a half ago, but his status remained the same: stable, but in a coma. It was a rainy day, sleet covering the courtyard and making the concrete walkways slippery. Keith and Nigel sat in the lounge playing chess and drinking flat Diet Cokes; as cold as the machine kept the sodas, they so seldom got the time to use it that sodas sat for weeks at a time. Chaplain Kennedy sat in his study, perusing some ancient volume. It was on this day that Nate decided to visit the high security wing.

He approached the gate that led to the North Wing, entering a passcode he had gotten from Nigel. The first thing he noticed was several guards pacing up and down the hallways; he never saw that many guards at once in the Central Wing where he worked.

The second thing he noticed was that all of the patients' quarters strongly resembled the old jail cells, only cleaner, with barred doors. He could hear one deep voice moaning and several others sobbing, a melancholy chorus of insanity. He began down the center of the corridor, glancing into cells and quickly looking away when his eyes met a wide-eyed crazy man's. He had never seen such a large group of people so far gone; it was so sad it was sickening.

He was caught off guard by an arm shooting through the bars on his left and he jumped to his right. Before his mind processed that that was a mistake, a hand got ahold of his coat sleeve and he tried to pull away, turning to see the crazed face of an unshaven man. He then noticed the man was holding something... a prison shank! He cried out as the man stabbed him under the ear, pulling the knife down along his jaw and barely missing his throat.

He felt two hands grab his shoulders and pull him back firmly. He saw a guard grabbing the patient's wrist; he squeezed it until the shank clattered to the floor. The patient was howling like some kind of animal and looking at Nate with eyes filled with hate. Nate felt himself continuing to be dragged backwards and was pulled into a room with black walls and several television monitors. A bright light flipped on and he shaded his eyes with his hand, squinting.

"Hold still," he heard a relatively deep voice say and a hand gently grabbed his chin, tilting his head to the side. Nate winced. "Doesn't look too serious." Nate looked around as the man released his chin. He was obviously a guard, in a navy uniform. With his back turned, Nate could tell he had short black hair. When he turned back, Nate could see intense dark blue eyes and dark stubble covering the lower half of his face. As he applied disinfectant to Nate's wound, Nate noticed his nametag read 'Miller.'

"Miller... Are you Dean Miller?"

"Yes, I am," the guard said, applying bandages to the cut.

"I'm Nate Grimfield... Chaplain Kennedy suggested I get to know you. I'm new here, well, newer."

"I see. Yes, I'm friends with the Chaplain. He mentioned you once... Wish we could've met under different circumstances." He wiped his hand on his pants. "What were you doing so close to that loon's cell anyway?"

"Something startled me... I jumped back."

"You'll learn not to be easily startled after working here for a while." Dean lifted one eyebrow. "The people are nuts... and I don't just mean the patients... I guess the place just rubs off on people, with its past and everything."

"You mean the riot?"

Dean started to laugh, but stopped himself. "Yeah, the *'riot.'*" Nate looked confused. "Nothing. I have to get back to work, as I'm sure you do as well Doctor. Need to fill out a report... I'm sure we will cross paths again, at least with the Chaplain."

Nate made his way back to the Central Wing and walked into his office. Nigel looked up as he walked in, "What happened to you?"

"Shaving," Nate lied.

"Good God Nate, that couldn't have come from shaving," Nigel said looking closer.

"It's really not as bad as it looks…" Nate's voice drifted off as he noticed a painting of a lighthouse on the office wall for the first time. The light was out and a grey-green fog covered the lower half of the painting. The sky was grey, much like today.

Nate came back to reality, noticing Nigel was still staring at him apprehensively. He rubbed the cut, wincing; it stung.

"There was an incident, in the high security wing-"

"Oh Jesus Nate, don't tell me you actually went down there!"

"I was curious."

"But it's terrible… Keith and I had patients there, I always hated it; the bars, all the guards. And most of all, the look in their eyes… like they weren't even human anymore."

~~~~~~~~~~~~~~~~~~~~~~~~~~~

Nate stood in front of the mirror, carefully pulling up the edge of the bandage on his jaw. Once it was completely removed, he looked in the mirror, turning his head. The cut was somewhat shallow, but ugly, with a yellow liquid seeping out. At least the bleeding had stopped.

"Ugly cut," a voice behind him made him jump. He turned to see Dr. Richardson, "I heard what happened; I assure you it is a rare occurrence that anyone is harmed here at Bright Dawn." As he stepped closer, Nate could see he had grown paler; his skin was slightly off-color and he had bags under his eyes.

"Are you feeling all right, Doctor?"

Richardson coughed. "Yes, fine, just feeling a bit under the weather. 'Tis a cold, it will pass."

Nate nodded, "Well I think I'll turn in. Good night, sir."

"Good night," the Doctor replied.

Once in his room, Nate lay down and quickly fell asleep, exhausted from the day's events. And he began to dream. He saw the same green sky as before and when he looked around him, he realized he was standing on some type of circular pedestal with railings around the edges. He looked over the railing, but could only see a few feet below him, due to the fog. Screams and roars erupted from below and he fell backwards onto the cold metal floor. He looked up to see a tall dark figure standing over him. He was dressed in black from head to foot and had several blood spattered knives hanging on a belt around his waist. He took one from his belt that resembled a kitchen knife, but was different in some way. He knelt over Nate, the screams and roars below deafening.

The figure put a finger to his lips. Nate was paralyzed; he wanted to move, but could not. The figure touched the cut on Nate's face, then gently grabbed the collar of his shirt, resting the knife on the side of Nate's neck, then slowly began to slit his throat.

Nate wanted to pull away, to scream along with those below him, but he was rooted to the spot, only able to feel the cold metal floor on his hands and through his pants, and the knife slowly slicing through his throat. He felt warm blood beginning to run down his neck to his chest. Suddenly the knife stopped its journey across his neck. He looked up to see the figure staring at something. All was still except for the ghastly noises below. The figure slowly turned back to Nate, taking the knife from his neck. Nate was breathing hard; maybe he could move now... The figure suddenly thrust the knife into his chest.

Nate sat up, gasping, his hand over his heart. He looked around the dark room, then grabbed his throat. No cut there, it had just been an awful nightmare. He fell back against his pillow, staring straight up at the ceiling. He began to doze off again when he heard a scream - *real* this time. He looked around, trying to figure out where it had come from. He stood and walked to the door, looking out into the hallway, but all was quiet and still. He went back to his bed and listened in silence a while.

"Maybe Dean was right, the place just gets to you," he finally said, laying back down.

~~~~~~~~~~~~~~~~~~~~~~~~~~~

Nate awoke to a knock on his door. "Coming," he said drowsily. After a few moments, whoever it was knocked again, harder this time. "I said I'm coming." He answered the door to find a middle-aged man in a suit holding up a badge.

"From what this says, you're Dr. Nate Grimfield?"

"Yeah, that's me. What's this all abou-"

"Where were you at approximately 1:30 this morning?"

"I was here in my room asleep."

59

"You were asleep the whole time?"

"I woke up once, but went back to sleep."

He jotted some things on his notepad, "Thank you," and walked down to the next door.

Nate looked down the hall and saw Richardson speaking with another man in a suit. He began down the hall, curious.

"No sir, I was in my room from 10:30 until you called. I think she's just confused about what she saw, after all it was so late, she must've been dead tired; you know, not in her right mind."

"Thank you for your time, Doctor." The man went to join his partner. Nate saw the door to the security checkpoint was open and Nurse Norris was sitting just inside. She looked as if she had been crying and was shaking her head slowly and staring at the floor. He looked around the hall; it was beginning to fill with curious doctors who had been disturbed. In the crowd he spotted Dean Miller surveying the scene, his hands on his hips, frowning pensively. He looked up, his eyes meeting Nate's. Dean lifted an eyebrow, cocking his head to look past Nate. Nate turned to see the men enter the security office, exiting once more within what could not have been more than a couple of minutes.

"Sorry for wasting your time, Doctor, we just have to take every call seriously. Protocol and all," one of the suited men said, shaking Richardson's hand.

"I understand, not a problem at all gentlemen."

Nate looked back at Dean. Dean watched the men leave, then sighed, and glanced back at Nate before exiting the wing. Norris walked out of the security checkpoint, still appearing to be in a daze. The other doctors had begun returning to their rooms to get dressed in proper work attire and Richardson was nowhere to be seen. Nate walked toward Nurse Norris; he had to know what all of this was about.

"Norris," she turned to him, "what in the world is going on?"

She looked into his eyes; he could tell she had been crying again, "Oh, Nate... it was terrible. I saw it... I saw it with my own two eyes, but nobody believes me."

"What? Norris, what did you see?"

"Dr. Richardson... I was up checking the patient dosages when I heard someone get off the elevator. So I walked down the hall and saw a light on in one of the therapy rooms... then I heard someone cry out and when I opened the door, there was Dr. Richardson, electrodes attached to his head... he-" her voice cracked, "-he was performing electroconclusive treatments on himself. I... I backed up, knocking something over and he saw me, but his... his eyes weren't right! And I ran, screaming, then grabbed the nearest phone to call for help... Oh, you've got to believe me! Every word is true, I don't care about 'sufficient evidence,' I know what I saw." She began to cry.

Nate put his arm around her. "There there now, I'm sure you saw something, but Dr. Richardson is a professional. He wouldn't perform those kind of tests on himself."

She slowly pulled away. "You-you don't believe me either..." She shook her head, then wiped her eyes and turned, walking away, her heels clicking with every step she took.

Nate looked at his watch; it was a quarter 'til seven. He went to his room and quickly pulled on some clothes and made his way to the courtyard, nearly slipping on the still frozen concrete. He entered the church and saw the Chaplain arranging things on the podium.

"Good morning, Nate. I thought you might be around." Nate stopped in mid-step; how had the Chaplain predicted his movements? "Dean was here just a bit ago. Told me about this morning and your little accident." He pointed to Nate's face.

Nate rubbed his cheek, then looked up at Chaplain Kennedy, "What do *you* think happened this morning?"

"I don't know," he stepped down from the stage and sat down on a pew. "Dean thinks there's more to the girl's story than meets the eye... but I couldn't say."

"What about the other incident?" Nate sat on the pew behind the Chaplain, voicing the real reason he had come.

"Other incident?"

"When we talked about the riot... you said that wasn't the only incident. What was the other?"

The Chaplain sighed, "Oh, yes, that... it must've been about 1946; I was nine years old. My father had come over from Ireland with his father years before and they had become leaders in the community, especially in the church... though at this point my grandfather was dead. Pelf used to be a coal mining village... until one day, when most of the men were in the mines, awful storm clouds were seen coming in off the bank of the lake. We all began inside as a thick fog filled the streets.

"Then, the wife of Jared Lukert, the lighthouse operator, came running down the street, screaming like mad. She heard something in the mines; some*thing* was down there with the men. The whole village went into a frenzy and Father finally got everyone rallied into the church. There was no rain or lightning that day… only thunder. When the fog cleared and the clouds lifted, my father and some other men who weren't already in the mines went to investigate. They were gone for several hours and when they returned, their faces were glum.

"All the miners were dead, they said… they closed down the mines. My father made me stay inside as they hauled the bodies to a cave just beyond the church and buried all the miners there, almost like a memorial to that day. Then they built a gate across the entrance of the cemetery. Nobody took flowers or paid their respects… it was strange.

"My father never told me about his time in the mines… the only thing he said was 'it always snows in Pelf to extinguish the fires of Hell.' The mines never opened again."

"Why didn't you stay in Pelf after your father died?" Nate found the story astounding, yet he believed every word.

"The people in Pelf's faith died long ago… perhaps even with those poor miners," he shook his head sadly. "Something was wrong that day… I had a feeling, even as a boy."

Chapter 5

"Dammit," Nate looked through his satchel one more time before looking up at Nigel. "Do you know if Mosher's carries razors? I seem to have misplaced mine."

"I don't know, never been in Pelf," Nigel shrugged, not looking up from his magazine.

"I'm sure he'll have *something* and I've got nothing." He stood, pulling on his coat. "I shouldn't be over half an hour." He began down to the elevator, but stopped in his room first to grab the key from Owen; he would ask him about that after his stop at Mosher's.

"Where're you off to?" Nate had one foot out the door, but stepped back at the sound of Mary's voice.

"Pelf."

"Dr. Grimfield… right?" She looked unsure of herself.

"Yes, Nate Grimfield," he smiled at the fact she had remembered his name.

She seemed pleased with herself for remembering too. "In a big place like this, it's easy to get names and faces mixed up. What're you going there for?"

"I seem to have misplaced my razor," he blushed; he was not exactly sure why.

"I see… I won't keep you any longer, Dr. Grimfield."

"That's all right," he smiled to himself, exiting the building and making the short trek to Pelf. He looked up at the sky; no storm clouds today, just grey-blue sky. He walked into Mosher's and began perusing the shelves and bins.

"Thought you left," he heard Mosher grumble.

"Yes, I did. But I'm actually here to buy something today, Mr. Mosher."

"Thank God!"

Nate found what he was looking for and as he was leaving, passed Bill Pratchett. "Hello Bill."

"Doc! Didn't see you there, how have you been?" Bill shook his hand.

"Good, good, and yourself?"

"Can't complain."

"Hey, do you know where Owen Rice is, I really need to talk to him."

Bill's smile shrank. "You don't know… guess word didn't get to Bright Dawn. Owen's missing; he has been for about a week now." Nate felt a chill go down his spine. "The odd part is his boat is still moored at the docks and from what anyone can tell he didn't pack up and go anywhere. It's weird…"

"Yeah… weird," Nate checked his watch. "Well, I really should be getting back to the hospital. Bye for now."

"Good-bye Doc."

As Nate made his way back to his office, he passed Keith's office and could hear him speaking heatedly. He stopped, trying to figure out what was going on.

"No… No, that's not it… Of course I want to spend time with you! I… I've told you to come spend time here several times… Babe, I need this job, I took it for both of us so we'd have the money- don't be like that… Well what the hell am I supposed to do, just leave and see you in Wisconsin!?… I can't just leave– babe- wait… Hold on, please, don't say that… I love you. I gotta go-… I gotta go."

Nate heard him hang up the phone and plop down in his chair, sighing. He stood there a moment longer, then went on to his own office.

~~~~~~~~~~~~~~~~~~~~~~~~~~~~

Nate stared at his blank computer screen, his head propped up on his hand, the dim glow illuminating his face. It was that time of the morning when there's nothing going on: too early for a break and no need to make rounds again, since you just did. The grey sky outside his office window made the morning seem even duller.

He dropped his gaze from the computer screen to his desk. He spotted the clipboard. *What is William trying to say?* He had not thought about it in weeks, but only now did a second question strike him: *who* had written the first question? But still more importantly was, what *was* William trying to say…

"Oh stop it," he thought, "*It doesn't mean anything, he's just a woman killer who plays the same dull notes on the damn piano every day, now vegetating upstairs; he wasn't saying* anything, *just more of his nutso bullshit.*"

67

"It's weird," Nigel's comment fit in oddly well with Nate's thoughts.

"What?" Nate knew it had nothing to do what he was thinking though.

"Keith... He left me this note... Here, why don't you just read it?" He slid the piece of paper - ripped from a spiral notepad based on its jagged top - across his desk. Nate took it and began to read.

"Hey Nigel – You'll never guess what I just heard Caulderstone talking about. Apparently he heard they're flying in a ton of Russian inmates straight off death row. He was going on about how they're dirt cheap and there is no paper trail to follow... I don't know if this is true or just a joke, since it came out of Reese's mouth, but you never know. Anyway, I'll see you in a couple of weeks after I get back from Wisconsin. –Keith"

"When did he give you this?" Nate continued to stare at the letter.

"Before he left."

"He's gone!?"

"Yeah... I thought you knew that. He went to see his fiancée in Wisconsin. He left an emergency number." Nate looked back at the letter. "It's nothing," Nigel took it back from him. "We both know Caulderstone isn't the most reliable source."

"Yeah..."

"Really, you okay?" Nigel asked, concerned.

"Yeah, I'm fine... so why did Keith just up and see his fiancée? It didn't seem like there was any notice."

"It was, er… an emergency."

Nate thought back to when he had eavesdropped on Keith while he was on the phone. "I see…"

"But really," Nigel waved the note, "it's nothing… Reese is just going on, like usual." He wadded it up and threw it away.

~~~~~~~~~~~~~~~~~~~~~~~~~~~

Nate could hear someone crying out in pain, or at least he thought it was some*one,* but it did not sound completely human.

"Hush now," he suddenly heard Richardson's voice, "you just hush…"

CLANG!

Nate jerked awake, staring up at the vent over his bed where the noise had come from. He lay flat on his back, perfectly still, staring up at the vent. He could hear the shaft creaking; there was something up there. He felt as though his heart was going to beat out of his chest. He saw something move just between the slats of the vent. And then something fell onto his bed sheets.

He clapped his hand over his mouth to keep from screaming and backed up until he was slowly sliding up the wall. He kept his hand to his mouth as he looked up at the vent once more. The creaking was becoming more distant. His eyes crept down to the dark object on his sheets. He leaned over and pulled the chain on his lamp. As light fell on it, he tightened his grip on his face as the night's dinner tried to make its way back up his esophagus.

What lay before him was bloody, and appeared to be a piece of flesh. His mind began to race: rats… at Bright Dawn? But the whole place seemed so clean. What if it was sick... rabies, maybe. He decided to tell Dean and the Chaplain about it, they would not look at him like he was crazy for thinking this prestigious establishment had rats.

He could still hear Richardson's voice in his head, clear as day. *"Hush."*

~~~~~~~~~~~~~~~~~~~~~~~~~~

Nate took a sip of coffee and quickly spit it out. Whoever had made this pot had made it far too weak and it was now cold. He dumped his mug and the pot in the sink. As he began boiling a new pot, Dean Miller walked in.

"Well you look like hell," he said, grabbing a bagel and taking a big bite. "'ow's yer face?" He mumbled through half-chewed bread.

"Better I guess," Nate subconsciously put his hand to his face and blushed; he had forgotten to put a bandage over it this morning. "The seeping has finally stopped."

Dean swallowed. "That's good." He turned to leave.

"Hey Dean!" Nate yelled a little louder than he meant to.

Dean turned back. "Yeah?"

Nate looked around to make sure nobody else was around; there was no one of course, it was still too early for most people. Nate was only awake because he had not been able to sleep after his ordeal. The sheet was in a messy ball under his bed and he had kept staring up at the vent, expecting blood to come raining down on him at any second.

"There…" his voice was hushed now, "there was something in the vent over my room last night."

Dean frowned pensively, "Something?"

"I… I think it was a rat."

"There aren't rats at Bright Dawn… You're sure you weren't dreaming it?"

Nate nodded.

"I'll poke around and see what I can find."

"Thank you."

Dean smiled, and then exited the lounge.

Nate sat down, drinking his coffee, trying to get the image of rats breaking into his room out of his head. He had heard stories, of how in New York rats would come into nurseries and feed on infants. Those stories had always terrified him.

He finally stood and headed to the office. There was a note stuck to the door:

"My office. Bring your clipboard.

-Dr. M. Richardson"

Nate went into the office and grabbed his clipboard. He made his way to the elevator, but suddenly slowed. The walls appeared to move and there was that annoying buzzing again. He looked up to see the light over the West Wing flickering.

"*Didn't Slim just change that bulb?*" he thought, staring at it in disbelief. He dropped his gaze to the rusty doors with the black grimy windows. The strobing light cast eerie shadows on the doors. His gaze continued down and stopped on something dark on the floor. He bent to examine it. It was a torn piece of blue fabric that looked like denim but felt like cotton. He stood back up and stared at the door for a moment before trying the handle. Locked; what had he expected?

He slipped the piece of fabric into his coat pocket and continued to the elevator. It dinged and he got off on the sixth floor. As he approached the office door, he could hear Mozart blaring from the other side and what sounded like someone banging their fists against the wall. He hesitated before knocking.

The banging stopped, but the music persisted for a little longer before he heard the slow, deliberate click of the power button and the music ceased. He could hear Dr. Richardson making his way across the room. The door handle slowly turned. Nate could hear a thumping noise, loud in the silent hallway. It took him a moment to realize that it was his own heart beating.

The door opened and Richardson looked at Nate, seemingly surprised, "Grimfield? I hadn't expected you so early… won't you come in?" He opened the door wider, then returned to his desk and sat down in his chair. Nate sat across from him.

"May I see your clipboard, Grimfield?"

Nate passed it over. He watched the Doctor remove the papers and put them onto another, newer looking clipboard. It was then that he noticed the thick bandage wrapped around Richardson's hand.

"What happened to your hand?"

"Burnt it in the kitchen, very clumsy of me." Richardson quickly withdrew his hand. It was then that Nate really looked at him. His eyes were sunken in his head, tired. His skin was an even sicker shade than when he had seen him in the bathroom and his hair seemed as if it had quickly begun receding and thinning, his face now clean-shaven.

He felt in his gut that the Doctor was lying about his hand. "Did you hear about the new lighthouse caretaker?"

"Oh, what was his name... Rice? What about him?"

"Well... he's gone missing sir. I was just wondering if - being the head of the facility and all - if you even knew about it."

"Yes, I know. I just didn't see any reason to trouble you all with it... don't worry Grimfield, local law enforcement says it's likely he just abandoned his post and I have to agree with them. There wasn't much to do in the old place and after all, he wasn't a native."

Nate sighed. Richardson seemed calm; unaffected by this man's disappearance. But Bill Pratchett, a native, had not seemed so calm about the situation.

"If you don't have any other questions, I'll be returning to my work now." Richardson stood, hinting that Nate had overstayed his welcome.

Nate stood and nearly shook Richardson's hand, but thought better of it when he looked at the thick bandage.

As he rode the elevator, he took the piece of fabric out of his pocket and looked at it once more. He remembered when Mosher had given him the key from Owen. He had said, *"He was in one hell of a 'urry. Looked all riled up and was carrying some kinda box."* He felt a chill making its way down his spine and looked at the fabric once more, rubbing it between his fingers before returning it to his pocket. What exactly was going on here in this nearly forgotten corner of Michigan?

~~~~~~~~~~~~~~~~~~~~~~~~~~~

"Crawling through the vent, eh?" Chaplain Kennedy said, replacing the candlestick he had been dusting. "Did you see what it was?"

"No, just the-" he cringed, "-flesh it dropped."

"You will have to do something about those sheets before they get ripe."

"I know…" Nate looked down, ashamed. "I'm just positive it was a rat. But Dean said there are no rats…"

The Chaplain laughed, "No rats? You think I've never seen a rat in here?" He motioned around the dim chapel. "Dean's a bright boy… Sees past most of the mask they put on this place… But he actually believed them about the rats?" His tone grew serious, "And who knows what's festering in that West Wing nobody goes in. You know that isn't all white walls and sparkling windows."

Nate nodded slowly. He sat in silence while the Chaplain cleaned. Nate took the piece of fabric from his pocket and began absently rubbing it between his fingers.

"With the mines… was that the only other incident?"

Chaplain Kennedy stopped cleaning, "Yes," he said slowly.

"Why did you tell me and Dean about the incidents?" He paused but the Chaplain made no move to reply. "Why doesn't anyone want the outsiders to know?"

"I told you because people go crazy," he shook his head sadly. "Not like the people in the cells... a different kind of crazy... They get taken in by this place. They find it easy to ignore those rusty doors. They're no longer interested in the outside. They are okay with all the white: the walls... the coats... the *snow*-" he stopped abruptly. "I feel safe here." He looked around the chapel with its wooden walls, colored windows, and lack of fluorescent lighting, "And as for your other question, it should be obvious; they don't want negative publicity."

Nate realized he was playing with the piece of fabric and quickly returned it to his pocket.

"I hear Redmoor has yet to improve," Kennedy changed the subject. "I prayed for him today." Nate wondered why the Chaplain would bring this up of all things.

"That's right, he-" Someone burst through the doors of the chapel, revealing that it was pouring rain outside. The figure fell in a heap on the floor, soaking wet. Chaplain Kennedy rushed to him; Nate stood back, waiting to see the face of their unexpected visitor. Kennedy rolled him over to expose the face of Dean Miller.

"Help me get him off the floor!" Kennedy took his shoulders, carefully resting Dean's head against his chest. Nate rushed over to grab his feet. They lifted him onto the nearest pew. "Get me a blanket!"

As Nate passed to get a blanket, he saw Dean was abnormally pale. He snatched a blanket from the end of the pew and quickly brought it. Chaplain Kennedy began using it as a towel to dry Dean off.

"Get that jacket off of him; he's sure to catch cold in these wet clothes." As he removed the jacket, he also realized the left sleeve was torn. He threw the jacket to the side and focused his attention on Dean. His breathing had evened out some and he was beginning to rouse. The Chaplain dried his hair and he opened his eyes, grabbing Kennedy's arm, his head rising, eyes wide, staring straight into Kennedy's. "It was... like a nightmare," he said breathlessly.

"What was, Dean?" Chaplain Kennedy asked in a warm tone.

Dean lay back down, squinting his eyes closed in a wince. He swallowed, then opened them again and stared at Nate as if seeing him for the first time. "It wasn't rats," his voice was thick, as though he was fighting tears.

"What?" Nate was caught off guard.

"Hold on," Dean closed his eyes again. "Let me catch... my damn breath." He looked at Kennedy apologetically for his language. "I did go... to check out your vent story," he winced again and Nate saw a tear forming in the corner of his eye. "There was a dried trail of... of... blood in the shaft, going either way. I got ahold of a blueprint to see where your shaft led... and one end was connected to the... the..."

"The what?" A chill racked Nate's whole body.

"The West Wing." Thunder clapped outside and lightning lit up the windows, casting colored shadows about the room. "I got a master key... I suppose it was an excuse." He chuckled scornfully,

"I'd always wanted to go in there… But I didn't find rats, I… I…" He stopped and swallowed, he was crying lightly now and his breathing had sped up again. He stared straight ahead, at nothing. "There were *people* in there." The words hung in the air. "But they weren't all right… something was wrong with them… I… they… one reached out to me, grabbed my coat sleeve. I almost felt sorry for him… until I saw his eyes… they were sewn shut, but I could see him looking at me through the stitches. I pulled back and then… I ran. I locked the doors behind me and tried to find you, but I couldn't find you, until I came here and then I guess," his speech was fast, slurred, his words running together, "the adrenaline just went out of my system and I collapsed… Oh God," he began to sob. "So wrong… there was something so wrong…"

Kennedy looked at Nate, meeting his eyes, and then turned back to Dean, "Calm down… you need to rest a little."

"But they were *there*!" he clutched Kennedy's shirt.

"I believe you," the Chaplain said earnestly and Dean relaxed, laying flat on the pew, closing his eyes, trying to shut out the horror he had seen.

Nate thought of Keith's note. He almost said something to the Chaplain, but something stopped him. He looked at poor, worn out Dean, then slowly exited the chapel to check on his patients.

~~~~~~~~~~~~~~~~~~~~~~~~~~~

Nate was walking down the hall, writing notes about the improvement of a patient when he ran into someone.

"I'm so sorry," he knelt to pick up the folders and clipboards now strewn across the floor, "I wasn't looking where I was-" he stopped short when he looked up to see Mary.

"That's all right," she took the pile of papers from him. "I wasn't really looking either."

He realized he was staring at her. He tried to stop, but could not; he hoped he was not blushing.

"I'd better get this to Richardson." She stood and he mimicked her motion.

"Yeah," he nodded and smiled at her.

As she walked away, he saw an exceptionally young security guard rushing down the hall. He nearly ran into Nate, his eyes straight ahead of him, never straying.

"Hey, watch it," Nate said, catching the boy's arm. His name tag read 'A. Rousseau.'

He stopped abruptly and turned to Nate. "Sorry sir, I-"

"Well where are you going in such a hurry?"

"North Wing. Guard didn't show up for duty, sir."

"You don't have to call me sir-"

"It's a sign of respect. Au revoir, sir."

Nate realized he, like himself, was a foreigner due to his French accent and insistence to call him 'sir.'

As odd - almost funny - as the guard had been, Nate felt queasy. Something was amiss. He checked his watch. Nearly lunchtime; he would visit the Chaplain to see how Dean was after a rest.

The rain from the night before had frozen over, making the walkways slick. As Nate entered the chapel, he saw the blanket Dean had used balled up at the end of the pew. Kennedy was nowhere to be seen; he must be in his office. He found him there, organizing books. The Chaplain always seemed to be making sure everything was in order.

"How's Dean?"

"He was fine when he left last night. Still a little shook up, but the color had returned to his face and he was fairly dry."

Nate nodded. His fist was in his pocket, closed around the piece of fabric. What was keeping him from telling the Chaplain? Did he still not trust him?

"I'm going to go see how he is." Nate wanted to tell the Chaplain then more than ever, but he could not. It was as though some invisible force was keeping him from telling.

"You should go do that," Kennedy replied. He had a sly grin, almost as if he knew Nate held something in that hidden hand.

"I... yeah," Nate turned to go.

"You can lead a horse to water, but you can't make him drink... just as a man can tell another a story, but he can't make him believe it." Chaplain Kennedy's words sent a strong sense of guilt through Nate. "Why're you still refusing to believe something is wrong here?"

Nate ran out the door, small snow crystals sticking to his hair. He slipped and fell, his backside hitting the pavement hard. He climbed clumsily to his feet and kept going until he was at the door,

79

then attempted to regain his composure. That was not the first time the Chaplain had predicted his moves or known what he was thinking.

He made his way to the North Wing. He would show Dean the fabric; ask him if that was what the people had been wearing. He entered the access code and turned into the security checkpoint.

"Whatchoo need?" asked a gruff man sitting with his feet propped up, chewing on a toothpick.

"I need to see Dean Miller. I'm Dr. Grimfield, it's very importan-"

"Dean ain't here. Bastard didn't check in dis morning."

A chill ran down Nate's spine. He suddenly remembered the young guard, *"North Wing. Guard didn't show up for duty, sir."*

"D-do you know his room number?" Nate found it difficult to speak; his mouth had gone dry.

"215, I think," the guard's tone changed, "say, whatchoo want him fer?" But Nate was gone, already nearly to the elevator. He rode down to the second floor and located room two-fifteen. He began pounding on the door.

"Dean... Dean, open up... It's Nate... Dammit Dean, answer the door!" He tried the knob but it was locked. "Dean..." his voice was pleading now, not demanding. "Open up..." He turned from the door, his back flat against the wall. He felt trapped. It was difficult to breathe, his chest was tight.

He arrived back on the third floor and quickly spotted a figure in full surgeon's dress. Even dressed from head to foot in white, it was unmistakably the figure of Dr. Richardson.

"Dr. Richardson," Nate felt bold; frazzled. The figure turned to him. "Dean Miller didn't report to his post today… Would you happen to know where he might be?"

"Yes, I know, I had to put someone in his place," the Doctor's welcoming tone was gone, he sounded almost annoyed, "but no Grimfield, I don't know where he is; if I did I would have sent him to his post."

"What about Owen Rice?" Nate wanted to stop, but he was so upset - so scared - that his tongue seemed to move of its own accord. "He's been missing for four weeks and now Dean Miller too?"

"Grimfield, as the head doctor here at Bright Dawn, I have much larger concerns than missing caretakers and guards who can't clock in on time. Will that be all?" His eyes burned into Nate's from behind the thick glass lenses and Nate suddenly had nothing to say.

As Richardson walked away, Nate made up his mind to do something else, something he now knew he should have done days ago. He would tell Chaplain Kennedy about his dreams and the fabric he had found outside the West Wing.

Chapter 6

"So you decided to come back." The Chaplain did not even look up as Nate entered his office.

"Dean is... gone."

"I know," Chaplain Kennedy looked at him. "But *you* had to know. You had to see for yourself the dark going ons - just telling you wasn't enough."

"I have dreams," Nate said quietly. "When I sleep here, I have... frightening dreams."

"What about, Nate?"

"Everything is dark... but, there is a green hue to... everything. People are always screaming and I can hear something else, like a roar. And... the last dream I had... someone tried to kill me," he was shaking his head and rocking back and forth.

"Who was it?"

"I-I couldn't see his face," Nate shook his head more definitely. "There was one dream that wasn't about the dark place."

"What was it about?"

"The doors to the West Wing."

"And what happened?"

"There was... some*thing* behind the doors."

Kennedy frowned pensively.

"And I found this outside the West Wing the other day," he extended his hand, offering the Chaplain the piece of fabric.

Chaplain Kennedy's expression became even more troubled. He took the fabric. "Thank you... You better get back to work... I need some time to think."

~~~~~~~~~~~~~~~~~~~~~~~~~~~

William Redmoor opened his eyes and looked around. Everything was blurry and he could hear a beeping; it echoed in his mind.

"Welcome back," he winced as a high pitched voice pierced the air, echoing strangely. "Do you know your name?" She shined a small light into his eyes and he recoiled again. He tried to move his hand to shield his eyes, but it was strapped down. "It's William," she clicked off the light and he could see that she was an African American woman, "William Redmoor. You've had brain surgery. You've been out for almost five weeks. You're better now, everything's gonna be okay. I am Nurse Norris." Her voice continued to echo when she spoke and he just wanted to cover his ears. "Norr-is," she said it more slowly. "How do you feel?" He did not answer. She looked over her shoulder, "He won't say anything, call Dr. Richardson."

~~~~~~~~~~~~~~~~~~~~~~~~~~~

Nate looked up from his paperwork to see Mary struggling with a large stack of files. He got up and went to his door.

"Here, let me help you with that."

"Oh," she looked surprised, "Dr. Grimfield... thank you."

"No problem," he smiled. "Where are you taking these?"

"To surgery, on the fourth floor." They got on the elevator and were silent a moment. "If you don't mind my asking, why are you here?"

"Excuse me?" he asked, confused.

"What made you come to Bright Dawn? We are so isolated and you are kind of a... city boy."

He shrugged. "It was the opportunity of a lifetime." The elevator doors opened, "Bright Dawn is known around the world and—"

They both jumped as someone started screaming. Nate shifted the files to one arm and caught Mary with the other as she fell against him, recoiling from the horrible wailing. Nate looked past her to see two guards leading William Redmoor to the elevator. He was in a straightjacket and screaming his head off, staring at Mary.

"Come on," Nate said quietly, guiding Mary out of the elevator. Redmoor was still screaming as the two guards led him into the elevator and the doors closed behind them.

"What was wrong with him?" she whispered, and then straightened, regaining most of her composure. "We need to deliver these." She headed off toward the surgical offices. A voice in the back of Nate's head said, *"What is William trying to say?"* but he shrugged it off and followed the clopping of Mary's heels.

~~~~~~~~~~~~~~~~~~~~~~~~~~~

Nate looked up from the patient assessments he was working on. "You hear Redmoor woke up this morning?"

85

"Yeah," Nigel continued doing an inventory of their patients' medications. "Heard he scared the hell outta Mary too. What happened exactly?"

Nate shrugged. "He saw her and just started screaming." He pushed his clipboard forward on his desk.

"Hey, where'd you get that?"

"What?"

"That clipboard," Nigel pointed, "we haven't been issued new ones in ages."

"Richardson gave it to me-"

Suddenly everything went dark. Nate heard something fall to the floor and small objects scattering; he assumed Nigel had dropped some pills.

"Can't see a damn thing - AGH!" Nate heard a crash and Nigel fumbling around in his desk drawer. He heard something click and then there was a narrow beam of light. As the light approached him, he could see Nigel holding a red plastic flashlight.

"I was a Boy Scout," Nigel grinned, "always be prepared." Nate laughed nervously, still shook by the sudden power outage. "Wonder what's going on," Nigel stuck his head out the office door and shined the light down the hall. When he came back in, he said, "Nobody… Guess they're all sticking to their offices like us. Hope the gates hold, the North Wing is the worst to keep contained with the power out."

"This happened before?"

"No, not since I've been here at least."

After about ten minutes, the lights came back on. Nate shielded his eyes, blinded by the sudden brightness.

Nigel turned off his flashlight, also shielding his eyes. Then he shrugged. "Guess it was just a bad breaker or something."

An alarm started and a voice came over the intercom, "Attention, stay where you are. The facility is being put on lockdown, code yellow. Patient William Redmoor has escaped. I repeat, remain where you are and stay calm, security personnel are apprehending Redmoor as we speak."

Nigel's eyes widened in fear as he looked at Nate.

~~~~~~~~~~~~~~~~~~~~~~~~~~~

Biff looked away from Katie as the alarm cut through the air. He had never heard that sound before, but he knew what it meant; one of the crazies was loose.

"We'd better get inside and lock the doors," Bill said, moving toward the door.

Katie began in the other direction, but Biff caught her arm, his gaze shifting back from Bright Dawn to her. "I have to get back to Vincent," she explained.

"He'll be fine as long as he locks his doors. Come on, when the alarms go off, we go in," Biff persisted. She reluctantly followed, Bill locking the door behind them and the three retreating to the storage room.

~~~~~~~~~~~~~~~~~~~~~~~~~~~

After Greg Mosher had set the deadbolt on his door, he shut off the lights as an added precaution, the only light what little bit of sun leaked through his window shades. He retrieved his shotgun from behind the counter and sat down in a chair he had dragged to the middle of the room. He sat facing the door, the gun lying across his lap. There was not a sound aside from his breathing and the rattling of his outdated heater. But soon even the rattling stopped. So had the alarm outside.

Mosher slowly stood and made his way to the wall and flipped the light switch. Nothing happened. The power was out again. He retreated back to his chair. Then he heard something move.

His head jerked in the direction of the sound and his eyes fell on the locked closet at the far end of the shop. It had been locked since he had acquired the place, with no key. Surely there could not be anything *alive* in there. He tightened his grip on his gun, sweat forming on his brow despite the increasing cold now that the heater was out. But then he heard it again, a scraping sound. He turned his whole body toward the closet, his eyes watching the gap between it and the floor alertly. The door creaked, as if something were leaning against it. Mosher pumped his shotgun, taking aim at the door.

———— End Part 1 ————

Part 2: It's Spreading

Chapter 7

"Holy shit!" Nigel felt his way to the door, locking it. "Redmoor is out there and we're all in the dark... What a nightmare..."

"Shh," Nate held up his finger. Nigel froze; they could see each other now that their eyes were adjusting to the dark. Nate stepped toward the door.

"No-" Nigel began, but Nate put his finger up again. He peered through their office door. He could only see darkness.

"Give me the flashlight," he whispered to Nigel. Nigel hesitated. "Give me the flashlight, I heard something."

Nigel stared at him a moment longer before hesitantly handing him the flashlight. He unlocked the door slowly. The lock clicked, loud in the silence. They both stopped breathing, standing perfectly still. Nate let out his breath gradually, then slowly turned the knob. He pushed on the door, but something was in the way. He pushed harder and it moved with resistance. He heard something dragging across the floor and took a deep breath before turning the flashlight on.

The light shown on a dark uniform. Nate moved the light along the shirt until he saw the flesh of a neck. He stepped forward, but almost slipped and caught the door for balance. He shined the flashlight down at his feet and saw his shoe immersed in a puddle of blood. He pulled back, but then he heard something move further down the hall. He did not see anything as he knelt over the guard and grabbed his sidearm before backing into the office.

"What was it?" Nigel hissed.

Nate swallowed. "A dead guard." He saw Nigel's eyes widen. "I don't know if staying put is the best idea... It is freakishly quiet out there," he motioned over his shoulder to the hall.

"... You're right, we gotta get outta here," Nigel's voice was rising in pitch. "But the place is on lockdown, we can't go anywhere, especially not without power."

"What do you mean?"

"I mean the doors are locked automatically, by the computers. You have to use the security computers to open them. And we don't even have the bypass code."

"Well there's gotta be a way out of here."

Nigel shook his head. "No... No, this is one of the most secure facilities in the world."

"We could at least get down to the first floor." Nigel looked doubtful. "Better than sitting around up here. And I have this." He held up the gun.

"Where'd you get that!?"

"Off the guard. Here," he handed Nigel the flashlight, "let's get to the stairs."

They stepped out the door and over the guard. They began down the hall when they heard a noise behind them. They both whipped around. Nigel shined the light all around the hall. Once again there was nothing. They were about to turn back when the grate flew from the wall vent, clanging against the opposite wall. Nate aimed his gun, his eyes trained on the open vent. He started to take a step toward it, but Nigel grabbed his shoulder and shook his head. Though he was curious, Nate knew he was right. He turned and followed Nigel down the hallway. They passed the elevator and Nate stopped abruptly.

"Nigel," he said in astonishment, staring at the unhinged, rusty blue doors, "come here." Nigel came to his side. The doors to the West Wing hung limply open. "I think I know a way out…" Nate thought about Kennedy's story. "There's an exercise yard through here."

Nigel thought a moment, then slowly nodded, "It's worth a shot."

They began into the West Wing. It was not white like the rest of Bright Dawn; the walls were a faded tan and the floor was a dark tile, both stained with age. Nate looked up at the leaky mildewed ceiling and nearly ran into Nigel, who had stopped dead in his tracks. Nate followed the beam of light with his eyes to where it rested on a body. He was bald, topless, laying face down.

"Wh-who is that?" Nigel's voice was as shaky as his hand, the beam of light dancing over the body. "I-I thought nobody'd been in here."

"Me too…" Nate frowned, remembering Dean talking about the people in the West Wing. Nate knelt beside the body, examining the pants he wore. They were a pale blue and when he touched them he knew they were the same fabric as the piece he had given the Chaplain. Pegged prosthetic legs extended from the torn pant legs. Suddenly, it moved. Nate jerked back, falling backwards onto his backside. The beam of light danced rapidly about the man; his bones cracked and groaned as he slowly stood, stretching his limbs. When he was fully erect, Nigel tried to steady the light on his face.

His eyes were sewn shut and his skin was a strange sick shade of pink. He gritted his teeth in some kind of smiling grimace and they were worn down as if he had been grinding them incessantly. Then there was another sound, a wet crackling. Nigel shakily moved the circle of light down the man's torso. Both men were petrified at what they saw.

Where his sternum should be, his ribs were split down the middle, jutting out of either side of his chest like teeth in a wide vertical mouth. And inside the rib-mouth, the heart, dangling limply and beating feverishly slow. Nigel's fingers loosened and the flashlight clattered to the floor, the light going out. They all remained perfectly still, the only sound the heavy, labored breathing of the man. Then a growl began to grow and gurgle in his throat, growing into a grotesque roar. An icy hand of fear gripped Nate's heart; that was the roar from his dream. Nigel fell to his knees, frantically searching for the flashlight. The thing's feet began to scrape across the floor, its breathing now a pulsing growl. Nate stumbled to his feet, the gun aimed into the darkness in front of him.

Nigel's hand closed around the smooth shaft of the flashlight. "Yes!" he exclaimed in breathless joy. He clicked it on. Nothing happened. He tried a few more times, then began banging it against his hand, "Come on… Come on!"

The light flickered, then died. The thing turned when it saw the flash and changed its course to Nigel. He banged the flashlight against his palm once more and it came to life. The thing was steadily speeding up.

"Hey!" Nate shouted and it turned back to him. He pulled the trigger, a bullet striking it in the shoulder. The force pushed it back, then it roared angrily and began running clumsily at Nate. He squeezed his eyes shut and pulled the trigger again. It cried out in defeat and slowly fell. Nate opened his eyes to see he had struck the dangling heart. It lay still and quiet. Nate crept toward it and nudged it with his foot. It remained limp.

"What... was that?" Nigel finally asked, sweat matting his hair against his forehead.

"I... I don't know. Some kind of medical experiment?" They both looked down at the dead thing. "Come on, we need to find the exercise yard."

They continued on until they came to a large open room filled with fairly modern hospital beds.

"What the hell..." Nigel shined the light around the room. "W-what was going on back here?"

"I don't know," Nate spotted a light on the far side of the room. He breathed deeply, trying to stay calm, and approached the room, his gun at the ready. Once in the room, he saw that the light came from a solitary candle that had nearly burnt all the way down, resting on a desk that was otherwise empty. The room appeared to be an old jail cell, with stone walls and a barred window. Other than the table, the only thing in the room was a wooden chair.

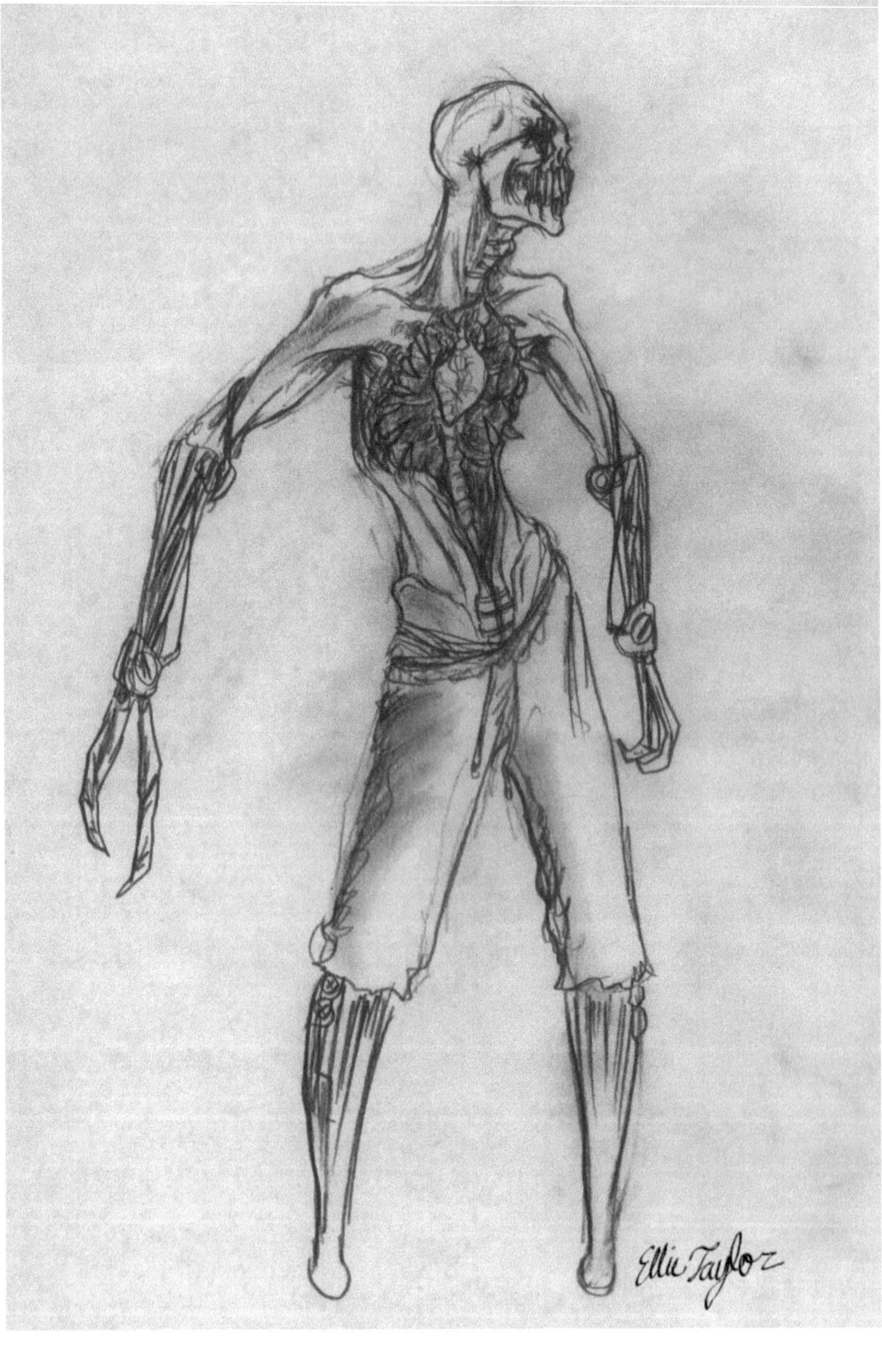
Ellie Taylor

"Nate," he turned to see Nigel standing by the wall, "look at this."

Nate walked over and saw what looked like a small child's drawing of a map in charcoal on the wall. At the end of the drawn trail, a brick was loose. Nate began to pull it out. At first, it stuck, but after some jostling, it came loose. Nigel shined the light inside the hole.

"There's a piece of paper." Nate reached into the hole to grab it and something touched his hand. He pulled it back quickly, clutching the paper. There was a huge spider on the back of his hand. He slapped it off and it scurried away into the shadows. He turned his attention back to the paper. It was yellowed and brittle with age; he began to slowly unfold it, and it crackled as he did so. Words were scribbled in atrocious handwriting: "Folks are gonna wonder why I dug a escape tunnel and never used it. The thing is cursed! I dug for three months, working night labor in the Boiler Room. Locked in all night, nobody but me. Check that gauge... mop the floors... DIG Cover the hole every morning. After ten feet I broke through to a natural cave. But there are things in that cave! I boarded it up and never went back. I rather die in this cell than go back to that tunnel."

"A tunnel... I never knew anything about a tunnel," Nigel frowned.

"This thing is old," Nate folded it and slid it back into the hole, "chances are no one knew it was here."

"Except for maybe whoever lit this candle."

They both fell silent. Nate looked out the barred window. All was white, covered in snow. And he saw a fence, with circular barbed wire wrapped around the top. He turned to Nigel, "I don't think we're exiting through the exercise yard... Is it possible that the tunnel is still there?"

"I-I don't know." Something creaked and they both turned to the door. "But I-I-I think we should g-get to the lower levels. Sa-safer down there." He was shaking.

~~~~~~~~~~~~~~~~~~~~~~~~~~~

The young guard shined the light around the bathroom. His name tag read 'A. Rousseau.' He was scared he might actually find what he was looking for: William Redmoor. The man that had killed his wife and daughter. Yes, he'd heard the story. He faced all of the stalls, "Anyone in here?" He heard nothing but the echo of his own voice.

He heard something move and jumped at his own reflection. But there was something else in the mirror. A tall, dark figure. Although dressed from head to toe in black, Rousseau recognized the man's stature as Dr. Richardson's.

"Oh, Doctor-" he turned and froze when there was no one behind him. He turned back to the mirror and saw only himself. "Dr. Richardson?"

He turned to his right as he heard someone begin to cry in the far stall. He approached the door slowly.

"Hello? It-it's all right. I'm not going to hurt you. I want to help." He opened the door. At first, darkness. Then a face emerged, with sickly wrinkled skin, white wisps of hair, and small eyes.

"Come on, get up-" Rousseau extended his hand. The face stopped crying all at once and became angry. It cried out in rage and spit in his face.

"Wait, no, ah, what the hell!?" Rousseau couldn't see, black ink-like substance had splashed into his eyes. He began to curse in French, wiping his eyes and taking steps backwards. Blinking severely, he finally opened his eyes.

He looked into the eyes of a new face, large yellow ones with a single black slash for pupils. The skin was mauve and almost scaly. The hair was wild and dark. Rousseau reached out in front of him to grab the face's arm. But there was no arm. He put both hands in front of him. Not only was there no *arm*, there was no body. He felt a warm wetness spreading across his pants and sweat running down his face, gathering around his lips. The face let out a scream, blood curdling, and Rousseau cried out as white sharp teeth and a dark spear-like tongue flew at his face.

Chapter 8

Nate followed Nigel down the last flight of stairs. They were passing through the lobby when he stopped. He could see a leg sticking out from behind the front desk. Fiery ice burned in his stomach.

"Nigel... Nigel, I think Mary's hurt," Nate started toward the desk. Nigel did not move. "Come on."

Nigel shook his head. "Nuh-uh... No. Not if Redmoor did to her what he did to his wife." He continued to shake his head. "I ain't going over there."

Nate held out his hand. "Give me the flashlight then." Nigel reluctantly handed it over. Nate slowly walked toward the desk. As he neared, he could see the floor was stained red and when he rounded the desk, he saw her once neat workspace was a wreck. He looked down at her and saw that she had a deep cut running from her collar bone to her stomach. She was bloody around her nose and mouth.

He knelt over her. "Mary?" he whispered.

Suddenly her eyes flew open and she put a finger to her lips, then looked around wildly. "It's still here," she struggled to say. She began to cry. "He tried to save me from it..." she sputtered.

"What is-" Nate stopped talking as he looked up and saw something large moving near the elevator. He shined the light at it and froze.

Its head was huge, lined with teeth as thick as a man's arm. It appeared to have been flayed and its eyes were held closed by chains that ran the length of its back, attached at the hindquarters. Its feet and hands were metal hooks. It was eating something on the floor, bloody meat caught in its teeth. Nate checked his gun; he had three bullets left. He was sure that was not enough to take it out.

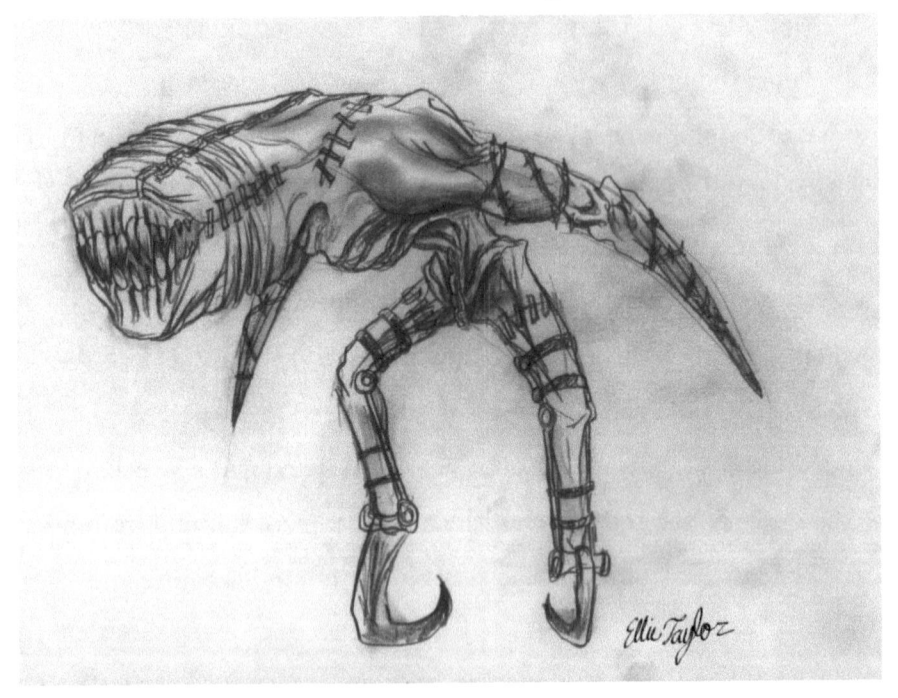

There was a security checkpoint just to the left of the elevator and the creature. If he could just get there without it noticing him, he was sure he could find more bullets. Or a bigger gun.

Mary coughed and blood flew from her mouth. She was not doing too well. He began to inch toward the checkpoint, crouched. The thing paused its eating. He froze, clicking off the flashlight. He waited for it to resume its meal, then continued to the door.

Once inside the checkpoint, he turned the flashlight back on. The floor was cluttered and the surveillance monitors were smashed. Propped against the desk he saw a pump action shotgun. He grabbed it and checked to see if it was loaded: two shells. He did not see any ammunition lying about and all of the drawers were locked. He would have to make those two shots count.

He leaned out the door to see that the thing was about ten feet from him. He took aim, training the light on the thing's head. He fired. The shell hit the monster in the side of the head. It jerked back, roaring in agony. It turned to Nate and stood, now much taller than him. He tried to pump the shotgun, but it was jammed. It began toward him. He tried to pump it again; still stuck.

Nigel had turned at the sound of the shot and roar. Now he saw the thing closing in on Nate. He was frozen in fear and defenseless. Finally he heard the shotgun re-engage, the pump a wonderful sound.

Nate smiled when the gun actually pumped. The monster towered over him. It raised its hooked hands and let out a defiant cry. Nate pulled the trigger. The cry ceased, replaced by a shocked moan. The thing retreated, running right past its meal and looking back at Nate once more and crying out angrily before disappearing to nurse its wounds.

Nate fell backwards in relief, dropping the gun and flashlight; the flashlight's plastic frame shattering as it hit the floor.

Nigel ran across the room to him. "What the hell was that!?" Nate continued to stare straight ahead, trying to catch his breath.

"*That* was not a medical experiment. That thing wasn't even remotely human!"

Nate's mind began working again. "I broke the flashlight." Then he remembered Mary. He stood and walked over to her. He took her wrist in his hand and checked for a pulse.

"Is she dead?" Nigel asked.

Nate nodded. Nigel began to cry. Nate put his hand on his shoulder, then turned back to what the monster had been eating. He guided Nigel toward it. He knelt, trying to feel for a badge or a nametag. A terrible squelching sound made Nigel wince as Nate's hand came in contact with the bloody flesh. He felt a belt. He walked his fingers slowly along it and found a flashlight strapped there. Obviously a guard.

As he turned on the light, Nigel turned away. The guard was a mess. Nate rolled him over with his foot. The face was bloody and torn, but familiar. He grabbed the badge on his chest and wiped away the blood. It read 'R. Caulderstone.'

"Oh Reese," he whispered sympathetically. He shined the flashlight around the lobby and spotted Reese's severed arm holding onto his gun. He took it from his rigid fingers. Nate checked Reese's belt for extra clips and found two. He handed Nigel Reese's gun.

"No," Nigel stepped back, "I don't do guns."

"You're gonna need it if we encounter something else." Nigel grudgingly took it and one of the clips; Nate kept the other.

Suddenly Nigel began fumbling in his pockets. He pulled out a small piece of paper and rushed to the phone. He began dialing.

"How will that work with the power out?" Nate asked.

"All the phones have an emergency battery. It just doesn't last long... Hopefully I have enough time to warn Keith not to come back." He grew silent, listening. "Dammit! He didn't pick up... Keith, this is Nigel. We have a situation here. Whatever you do, don't come back to Bright Dawn-" he could no longer hear air noise through the receiver. He slowly set the phone down, "I don't think the whole call got through..."

"I'm sure he heard enough. So how do we get to the Boiler Room?"

~~~~~~~~~~~~~~~~~~~~~~~~~~

Nate pulled his lab coat tight around himself. With the power out, it was beginning to get cold. They took the door labeled 'BOILER,' which was hanging loosely open. Large generators stood all around the room; silent sleeping giants.

"The note said it was down here." Nate began shining the flashlight between the boilers. The third gap he tried revealed a hole lined with shattered boards. "Gonna have to crawl through this part." Nate got down on his hands and knees and crawled into the tunnel.

He could see the larger cave ahead that the old inmate had written about. His hand touched something, a piece of paper. He wrapped his fingers around it and continued crawling. Once in the larger cave, he sat on a rock ledge jutting out of the wall and shined the light on the piece of paper. It was a postcard, reading 'Welcome to Paradise' with a picture of three hula dancers and a woman playing a ukulele on a beach. He flipped it over and saw a scrawled message. "For God's sake, get out before it's too late. Things are going to get much worse. –William." William? William Redmoor? He folded it and shoved it in his pocket, then he looked around the cave that tunneled through the blue, permafrost rock. Nigel emerged from the tunnel and they both looked down the path carved into the rock.

"Only one way to go..." Nigel shifted nervously.

"Let's go," Nate could see his breath come out as a puff of smoke in the cold cave air.

As they walked, the sounds of their shoes echoed throughout the cave; it was silent otherwise. Nate was getting tired of quiet, the fact that they had not encountered another living person, despite their short encounter with Mary, bothered him. And William had been this way; that could not be good if it was William *Redmoor*. Nigel began to slow, but Nate trudged on. His eyes were tired, his knees ached, but he kept on; walking had become an automatic motion. The need to survive pumped strong in his veins.

"Look," Nigel pointed ahead of them.

Nate's eyes focused, he had been walking in a trance. Ahead he saw a door built into a wooden wall. A door at the end of the cave? This whole situation got stranger and stranger. When Nate stopped in front of the door, he realized he was out of breath. He took a moment to regulate his breathing before trying the door. It did not move when he pulled. He pushed and the door creaked open. Nate shined the light around to see where they were. He recognized the bins along the walls. They were in Mosher's General Store.

"I know where we are..." Nate's eyes wandered around the store. Some of the bins were overturned. "We are in Pelf." The flashlight fell on an overturned chair in the middle of the room. "Mosher!... Greg Mosher! You in here?" Nate began across the shop, the floorboards creaking, "Mosher..."

Blood was splattered across the wall. Nate rounded the counter. There lay Mosher, ripped up pretty bad. His eyes were wide and staring. One hand clutched his shotgun; the other was in a claw, as if he had been reaching for something.

"Oh God, I think I'm gonna-" Nigel turned quickly and ran to a corner of the shop, and Nate could hear him vomiting. Nate tried to ignore the smell of blood and beer, and shined the light across the counter. The cash register was overturned and blood was smeared across the surface of one of the counter drawers. Nate tried to avoid touching the blood, but it was nearly impossible. Once he had opened the drawer, he shined the light inside, where he found two boxes of shotgun shells.

"Nate..." Nigel sounded drunk, "I... I don't take blood... too well... Ah damn." Nate saw him clutch his chest. "I think I'm having a panic attack."

He suddenly collapsed, his hand still over his heart and he was beginning to hyperventilate. Nate rushed over to him. "Hey hey hey, calm down. Breathe, Nigel, breathe." He looked back at Mosher. He needed the shotgun. "Just breathe... Nigel, close your eyes and think of a happy place, a good place - Kansas! Think about Kansas. Now hold this." He slid the flashlight into Nigel's hands. "Just aim that straight ahead and think about Kansas… Breathe, Nigel." He headed across the room, the light reflecting off Mosher's red blood. That was the whole purpose of making Nigel close his eyes; he knew Nigel could not take the blood. "You breathing?" He heard Nigel mumble, but it sounded like he said, 'Yes.' "Good. Kansas…" He grabbed the gun from Mosher's stiff fingers; rigor mortis had already begun to set in. He began to sing under his breath, "London Bridge is falling down, falling down, falling down…" He opened the drawer and grabbed a box of shells, "London Bridge is falling down," he felt his knees weakening as he headed back to Nigel, "My… fair… lady." He began to cry and he sat down, leaning against the wall, cradling the gun in his arms. It was like he had been on auto pilot and was just now getting in touch with reality. Mary was dead. They were all dead. He was holding a dead man's gun. "My fair lady…" he sniffed, wiping his eyes on his sleeve.

"You okay?" Nigel's voice was weak.

Nate tried to steady his voice. "You're in Kansas." She was bloody, she'd been so bloody. "Lovely, lovely Kansas…" It had flown out of her mouth when she coughed. "Breathe." He stood and continued to Nigel. He turned the light away from Mosher and wiped his eyes once more. "You breathing?"

"Yeah." Nigel seemed calmer, almost on the verge of sleep.

"You can open your eyes now."

He did, looking up at Nate. "I used to suffer from panic attacks before I worked at Bright Dawn… They stopped for a while, that was the first in a long time… It was just… too much."

"It's okay," Nate put his hand on Nigel's shoulder. "Think you can stand up?"

"Yeah…" Nate took his hand and Nigel stood, his legs still wobbly, but he grew steadier after a moment. "Yeah," he said more confidently.

Nate slid the pistol into his pants and loaded the shotgun. Then he slowly opened the door. Everything was dead silent; it was so quiet that he could hear the snow falling. All of the windows were dark and some were broken. Splotches of snow were dyed red with blood. But the worst had yet to come. The fountain at the center of the town square was piled several feet high with human bones. Nate looked toward the village gate and a chill rolled down his already frozen spine. Now he knew why to enter or leave the village, you had to pass through a large, peculiar gate. It was now closed and the fort-like fences were too high to climb. Nate looked past the fence to the sign that read 'Welcome to Pelf.' There were three long, jagged scratches across the words.

"Where-where is everybody?" Nigel looked lost; Nate remembered what Owen had said about doctors seldom being seen in Pelf. Chances were that he had never been to the village.

"I don't know." Nate looked out across the town. He desperately wanted to see another living human being, but the likeliness of that was dwindling.

A terrible scream cut through the air and suddenly Nigel was no longer beside him. Nate looked up to see him being carried away by a flying skeletal woman. Nate took aim with the shotgun. The thing was out of range, but he had to try. The shot erupted and she cried out in surprise, dropping Nigel into the snow below. Red was already spreading across the shoulders of Nigel's white coat. He groaned as he sat up. The witch was coming full circle to grab him again. She had blue translucent skin pulled taut over her bones and dark hair falling into her hideous face, which housed a wicked smile of jagged teeth, a rotted pug nose, and glowing red eyes. Her long fingers resembled daggers, reaching out for Nigel as she flew toward him.

BLAM! A shot rang out. Then another, followed by continuous shots until the dull clicking of an empty gun sounded. She cried out in defeat, crash landing and sliding across the snow. Nate looked up to see Nigel standing, his arm extended straight out in front of him, his hand clutching his pistol, a new look of focused determination on his face.

As Nate approached him, he could see that Nigel was trembling and he stiffly lowered his arm and winced, grabbing one of his bleeding shoulders.

"Bitch tried to kill me…" He grabbed Nate's shoulder for support and they both turned to look at her.

She began to flicker and her blue skin melted away. She now wore a pink blouse and black skirt. Her clawed feet now wore small black pumps and her messy hair twisted into a blonde bun. Her red eyes remained open, forming sockets and turning blue, her skin now a very human shade of pink. For a moment, Nate could have sworn it was Mary.

"Oh God…" Nigel's voice was unsteady. "That… that's Elizabeth Redmoor."

"Redmoor…?"

"William's wife… I recognize her from the pictures," Nigel stared down at her, "and I… killed her…" The gun slipped out of his fingers and landed softly in the snow.

Nate pulled back the torn fabric on Nigel's coat to examine his shoulders. "These cuts are pretty deep."

"If I can get cold enough, I won't feel it." Nigel pulled away from Nate and knelt, grabbing a handful of snow. He pressed it against his shoulder and cried out. "Damn, that stings!" He treated the other shoulder, then looked up, "Doesn't look like we can get past that gate… You've been here before; is there another way out?"

Nate thought a moment. "There are the docks."

Chapter 9

The two started across the snow, Nigel following Nate. They passed the Great Lake Inn. All of the windows were dark. Nate hoped Vincent and Katie were locked up somewhere safe.

They reached the docks. A chain-linked fence topped with spiraled barbed wire enclosed the area. A locked gate closed them off from the rest of the lake. Nate wondered how he had not realized how much Pelf looked like a prison complex when he had lived there.

Nate looked across the docks and spotted the Pratchett Brothers' shop. He remembered seeing them hauling large boxes out of a back room when he had first arrived. Maybe they had coats, furs, or medical supplies - something.

"Come on, I think we might be able to find something to help us in there." Nate pointed to the building.

"Will there be any more dead people in there?" Nigel's speech was slightly slurred; he was beginning to weaken from loss of blood.

"No," Nate lied, for he did not know what to expect inside the warehouse.

They carefully walked across the docks, trying not to slip on the snow-covered ice. Nate tried the door. It was locked. He threw himself against it. It creaked. He slammed against it again, but it still did not budge. He was about to ram it again when he saw the knob begin to turn. He stopped and stared at it, unable to move - unable to breathe. The door began to creak open and Nate tightened his grip on the shotgun. The head of a shovel came into view and then Bill

Pratchett stepped out, ready to swing. He froze when his eyes met Nate's.

"Doc?" he said breathlessly, surprised and relieved.

"Bill?" Nate said, equally surprised.

"Who is it?" Nate heard Biff's voice from inside.

"Nate Grimfield and… some other guy," Bill yelled over his shoulder. He turned back to Nate, lowering the shovel. "You two get in here." He opened the door wide enough for them to pass through, and then quickly locked it behind them.

It was warm inside the building. Nate looked around and noticed a propane stove.

"Nate!" Katie's voice rang out and she emerged from the darkness with a flashlight trained on him. She hugged him, smiling. Then her expression turned serious. "What happened to your face?" She rubbed the cut; her fingers were cold despite the warmth of the warehouse.

"Just an accident at the hospital," he smiled in spite of himself. He felt a swelling of happiness within him; others *were* alive.

"What the hell is going on out there!?" Bill's voice was loud and blunt. "We only go on lockdown when something is wrong at Bright Dawn."

"A patient escaped," Nigel replied.

"And who the hell are you anyway?" Biff shined his flashlight in Nigel's face.

"Not that it matters," Nigel put his hand up to shield his eyes, wincing when he moved his shoulder, "but my name is Nigel Brauer, I work at Bright Dawn with Nate."

"Look!" Nate said loudly, catching everyone's attention. "People are dead and I don't think the most dangerous thing out there is Redmoor."

"What do you mean? Who's Redmoor?" Biff crossed his arms.

Nate and Nigel exchanged a look. "There are… *things* out there." Nate paused, thinking of what to say. "They aren't people… Look at Nigel's shoulders," he pointed to Nigel.

Biff slowly uncrossed his arms and walked over to Nigel. Nate saw him hesitate when he saw how red the top of Nigel's once white coat was. He carefully grabbed a strip of cloth and shined the flashlight on Nigel's ripped flesh. He looked at Bill, glanced briefly at Katie, then looked back at Bill before stepping back.

"Do you think a person did that?" Nate asked.

"I don't know," Biff said quietly, looking at his feet.

"Look, the point is, it's not safe here. We need to get out of here." Nate looked between the brothers.

"Can't," Bill said quickly, "we are on the same power grid as Bright Dawn. As long as the power's out, those gates aren't opening."

"You've lived here your whole lives," Nate said pleadingly, "is there truly no other way out?"

Biff looked at Katie, then back at Nate, shaking his head sadly. "No… there's not." He and Bill exchanged looks; looks of

115

hopelessness. They were trapped here and the propane would not last forever.

"Did you find any other survivors?" Bill sounded as though he were fighting off tears or trying not to throw up; maybe both.

"No," Nigel replied.

"But we didn't look everywhere," Nate added.

Bill looked around the room at everyone. "Then I guess it's time we start lookin' …"

"And Owen?" Nate asked.

"Nothing." Biff continued to stare at his feet.

Nate thought back to Mosher's message. Owen had been carrying a box. What was in that box? And why had he left Nate the key to what he assumed was his boat?

"I am going to search his boat," Nate stated.

Biff started to say something, but Katie cut him off, "We need to go to the inn… I have to know if Vincent's all right."

"If there *are* monsters out there like you said, do you really think it's a good idea to split up?" Bill said, looking between them seriously.

"We need to get out of here. I think the only way we'll do that is if we cover more ground," Nate reasoned.

Bill slowly nodded, "All right. We'll go to the inn, and you go to the boat. Then we all come back here."

"You're going to need something to defend yourself out there," Nate said.

Bill held up the shovel in his hands. Biff went back to the corner he had been standing in and retrieved a sledgehammer leaning against the wall and picked up a nail gun, handing it to Katie. He then went over to a desk by the wall and began rummaging through the drawers and pulled out a protein bar.

"Here," he handed it to Nigel, "you look like you could use this. I'm sorry we don't have much else to offer you two…"

"Thanks," Nigel took it, putting it in his coat pocket. "I'll save it for later."

Katie took Nate's hand in hers and squeezed it. "Be careful."

"Same to you." He let go of her hand and turned to Bill.

Bill took his hand, shaking it. "Good luck, Doc."

"Good luck to you too," Nate nodded to Biff and then walked past them out the door, Nigel following. He looked back over his shoulder adding, "And Mosher's dead," then began across the snow.

"Nate… wher-where are we going?" Nigel's speech was even more slurred than before and he nearly fell, his knees buckling.

"To find Owen," the wind picked up and Nate had to yell over it, "or try to find out where he went!" Nigel's eyelids began to flutter. "You need to get back where it's warm and rest! I never said you had to come with me!"

"What!? And let you go off alone?" He looked directly into Nate's eyes. "If I hadn't been there for that witch to pick up, she would've grabbed you. Then who woulda shot you down?"

117

Nate could not argue. He sighed, looking at the streaks of now freezing blood on Nigel's coat. "Fine," he said, "but eat that stuff Biff gave you, you need the energy."

Nigel smiled, relieved that Nate was letting him come with him. He ate and they continued across the snow.

~~~~~~~~~~~~~~~~~~~~~~~~~~

Keith sat up in bed, putting on his glasses. The woman laying beside him rolled over. "Where're you going?"

"Restroom," he replied quietly, standing, the hardwood floor cold under his bare feet.

As he returned from relieving himself, he noticed the light flashing on the answering machine. He pressed the button and the computerized voice of a woman spoke.

"You have one unheard message. First unheard message," the voice changed to that of Nigel Brauer, "Keith, this is Nigel, we have a situation here. Whatever-" The message cut off and the robotic woman gave him the option to replay the message. He stood a moment in silence before walking back into the bedroom.

He slid his briefcase out from under the bed and grabbed some clothes out of the closet, including his white lab coat with 'McDonnell' embroidered on the right breast pocket.

"What're you doing?" The woman sat up, disoriented.

"Bright Dawn called," he answered, not looking up.

She blew her breath and rolled her eyes, "You're on vacation."

"I left that number for emergencies only." He looked at her seriously.

"So Bright Dawn's more important than me?" she added as he began tying his shoes.

"Yes- I mean no- it's just... I need this job, Louise."

He stood, grabbing his briefcase. She looked at him, shaking her head. "I used to think you were so smart, but it's a good thing you didn't become a cardiologist, because you know nothing about the heart." He turned to leave. "See, I know all your fancy damn terms!" she yelled after him.

"I love you," he said quietly before walking out the door.

~~~~~~~~~~~~~~~~~~~~~~~~~~~~

Nate wrapped his arms around himself, shivering. Even though the wind had died down, the cold had gotten down into his bones. He tried to think back to the warm summers he had spent at the university, the days when he had jogged around the campus with the sun shining on his face. But now the sun was down and snow fell all around him. It seemed like those days had been years ago. Even in the dark it was not hard to see, white snow covered everything, illuminating the silent world around them.

"Look," Nigel pointed to the lighthouse. Owen's house was not far, just down the slope from the tower.

Nate stepped forward and the snow dissolved into a grimy metal floor, the snow banks now walls that matched the floor, and the sky was filled with billowing green clouds. Nigel looked to Nate, horrified. There was a roar and they looked to see more of the zombies surrounding them, their chests snapping hungrily at them. A fog was beginning to curl around their ankles and slowly rise. "*We all began inside as a thick fog filled the streets,*" Chaplain Kennedy had said.

"Quick!" Nate pointed at the ominous tower that had been the lighthouse. "Get inside!"

As Nigel opened the door, a large floating fleshy ball wrapped in chains exploded, covering him in green slime. He cried out, but started up the stairs, Nate close behind. When they reached the top, Nigel swung the door open and ran onto the observation platform. Nate followed but stopped short, gripping the doorway. He was standing on some type of circular platform surrounded by railings. Roars erupted from below him. This was the place where he had been murdered in his dream.

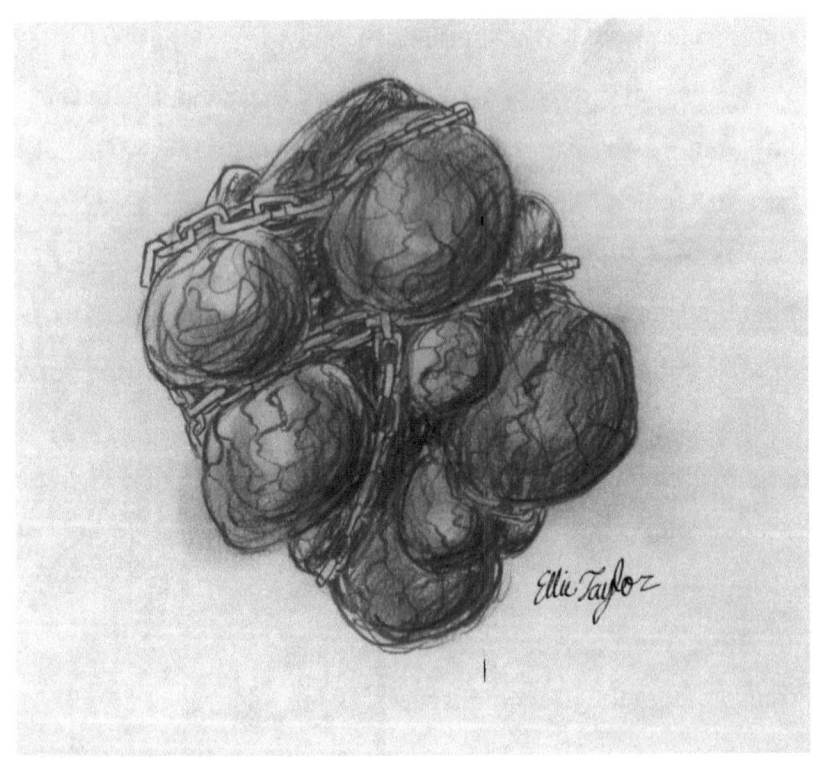

"What?" Nigel turned to see Nate frantically searching the room with his eyes.

"I... I've been here before."

Suddenly they could hear terrible feedback and Nate looked up to see a speaker attached to the ceiling.

"Dr. Nate Grimfield," the Doctor's voice sent a chill through Nate, "Nigel Brauer... Welcome to *my* Garden of Eden."

Nate looked down at the floor and saw an arrow drawn in blood pointing out over the railing. He leaned over to look, but could only see the thick green fog. Then the green faded back into white and they were in the lighthouse, surrounded by Pelf, no zombies below them. The slime on Nigel turned to dust. Nate squinted into the night and saw he was looking at the mine shaft Owen had pointed out to him.

"Nate," he turned to see Nigel pointing at where the bloody arrow had been, "look."

Nate knelt to see another postcard from Paradise. He flipped it over: "It's spreading like cancer. Hurry!" Once again, it was signed 'William.'

"What does it mean?" Nigel asked.

"I don't know..." Nate put the postcard in his pocket with the first. "Let's get down from here."

"And what was all that back there?" Nigel's voice went up in pitch, "All the metal and clouds and... things!"

"I don't know." Nate continued toward the mine.

"It was like... we weren't even *here* anymore." Nate moved a large plank of wood blocking the entrance to the mine. "Hey, what're you doin'?"

"The arrow that was drawn in blood, it pointed to this mine. Owen went here before he disappeared."

"And he didn't come back," Nigel took a step back.

"We don't know that... I'm going in, Nigel," Nate grabbed the flashlight out of Nigel's frozen fingers, "and you can't stop me."

Nigel stared after him, dismayed. A strange sound, like an animal being electrocuted rang out from behind Nigel. He spun around and saw something leaping toward them. As it neared, he saw it looked like a large tick, with two arm-like appendages ending in claws extended in front of it and a mouth full of gnashing teeth. Nate retreated into the mine. Nigel remained rooted to the spot, unable to move. He could feel his heart pounding as he reached for his gun, but there was no lump in his pocket. He looked around frantically and spotted it laying in the snow beyond the creature. He felt a scream growing in his chest, but it caught in his throat.

A shot sounded behind him and the thing stopped a moment, hissing angrily. It screeched and leapt at Nigel. He closed his eyes, putting his arms up to shield himself.

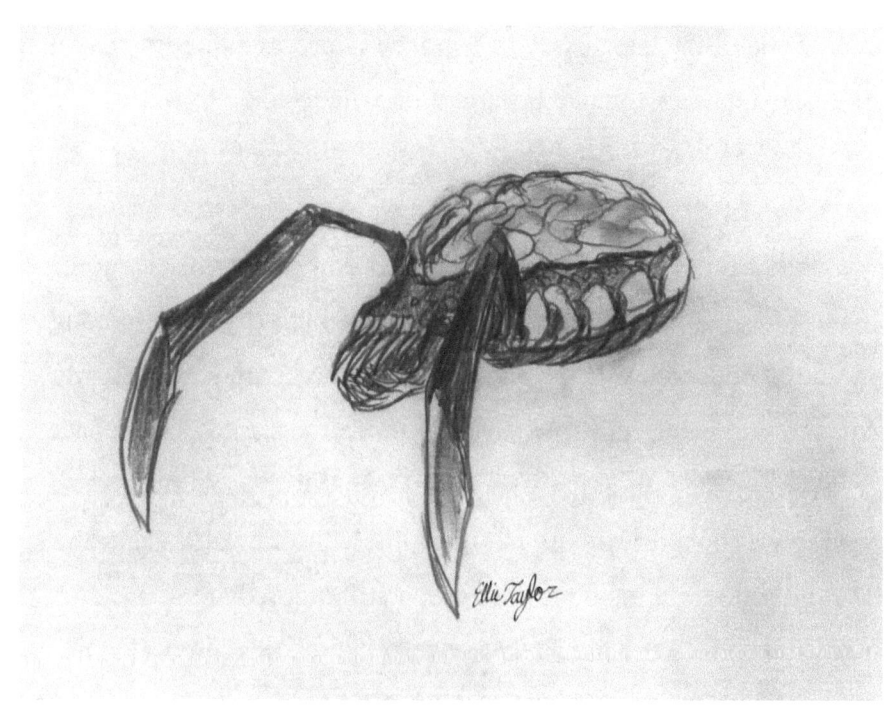

"*I'm going to die a coward,*" he thought, waiting to feel the claws cut into him. But there was another shot and the teeth did not bite into him; the claws did not gouge his body. He opened his eyes and slowly lowered his arms. The thing lay on its back, its legs curled inward like a giant dead spider. He looked back at Nate.

"You were right back at the docks." Nate said decisively, "We need to stick together."

Nigel nodded in agreement and they looked at the monster one last time before entering the mine. It was the same as the tunnel they had entered Mosher's General Store through, the rocks blue with permafrost. The cavern was small, containing a wooden shed, most likely for storing equipment, and a lift that led down. As Nate shined the beam of the flashlight across the lift, he noticed a piece of paper stuck to one of the supports. He removed it and attempted to read the writing; it appeared to have been written with a shaky hand.

"STAY AWAY! This place is cursed. No one should see what I have seen. I will make sure of it. This elevator leads to somewhere unnatural. Somewhere evil. Stay away. I don't know what's going on, but I'm not staying to find out. If it's the battery you're looking for, you're out of luck. I have taken it with me. I am leaving in my boat, and will never return. I suggest you do the same! –Owen Rice."

Nate frowned, thinking. The box Mosher had seen Owen carrying was not a box at all, but most likely the elevator's battery. But if he had left in his boat, why was it still moored at the dock? And why had he left Nate the spare key if he was leaving? Had he known something would happen to him? Was that why he had bothered to leave this note?

"I thought you said he was missing…"

Nate shook his head. "His boat is still here."

~~~~~~~~~~~~~~~~~~~~~~~~~~

Bill tried the door to the inn again as Katie and Biff peered through the windows.

"It's definitely locked, not just stuck." Bill stepped back from the door.

"Did you try knocking?" Biff asked.

"No, you idiot, I didn't try-" *CRASH!* Biff brought the sledgehammer down on the door. It bowed inward but did not break. He lifted the sledgehammer and swung again. The door splintered and Biff reached through the hole and unlocked the door.

"That's knocking…?" Bill said in exasperation and he followed Biff inside. They could hear one of his records playing from behind the counter.

"Vincent!" Katie called.

"Hoover!" Bill yelled up the stairs as Katie bounded behind the counter. Vincent's records were scattered across the floor and his stool lay overturned. Katie leaned to read the sleeve for the record on the player: 'Santo and Johnny.' She turned to her left and screamed. Vincent lay on the floor, his eyes staring at the ceiling, his right hand in a claw over his chest, his face frozen in a rictus of terror.

Biff hurried behind the counter because of her scream and she grabbed him, burying her face in his shoulder. Biff looked past her to see the dead Vincent Hoover, his hand clutched over his heart.

"*He always was excitable...*" Biff thought sadly.

There was a sound from upstairs and everyone's heads jerked up, looking at the ceiling. The brothers looked at each other. Biff released Katie and slowly set up the overturned stool, motioning for her to sit on it. She shook her head violently; they were all afraid to speak since they did not know who or what was upstairs. Biff gave her one last pleading look before heading up the stairs, Bill and Katie not too far behind. Everything was a mess: overturned chairs, broken lamps, rips in the expensive leather furniture. Biff approached Room 201 and opened the door slowly. It creaked. The room was empty, the pillows and bed sheets thrown to the ground. He edged his way down to Room 202. Holding the sledgehammer at the ready, he creaked the door open. Same as the last.

He turned back to Bill to say something when two hands gripped the handle of the sledgehammer, pressing Biff back against the wall. An angry face roared in his; its breath reeked of decay. Two green eyes peered at him through stitches holding the lids shut. Its heart pumped between large vertical jaws.

"Bill!" he cried out. "Get Katie out of here!" He pushed the thing back into the room.

"No!" Katie tried to raise the nail gun, but Bill caught her shoulder and pulled her toward the stairs. He got a better grip on her by wrapping his arms around her waist in a bear hug and carried her down the stairs kicking and screaming. Once they were outside, he collapsed under the awning.

"You left him!" she yelled angrily, hitting Bill's chest. "You just left him!"

"No." Bill tried to catch his breath, standing, "I did what he told me to. Now you stay here," he said seriously before running back inside, picking up the shovel he had dropped at the bottom of the stairs.

Biff and the thing circled each other, now in the second floor lobby. Biff swung but missed; the sledgehammer was too cumbersome. He looked around for something better to use. It lunged forward, grabbing the sleeve of his letter jacket. He dropped the sledgehammer and punched the thing in the face with his free hand and it released him, calling out in surprise. Biff heard a clang and saw the shovel slam against the side of the monster's face, knocking it to the ground. Biff grabbed the sledgehammer and dragged it across the floor until he stood over the shocked beast. He raised the sledgehammer above his head and brought it down on the zombie's gaping chest cavity. A roar died in its throat and it lay still. The brothers looked down at the thing, breathing hard. Then they heard more noises up on the third floor.

"More of them?" Bill gasped.

"Let's get outta here; we can't take all of them."

"They'd just follow us; we can't just lock them in since *someone* decided to knock the door down."

Biff set his jaw, looked up, and began to nod slowly, "We're gonna have to kill them then." He ran down the stairs and Bill followed.

"What the hell are you doing?"

But Biff was not listening, he was digging through Vincent's storeroom. He picked up a jug of motor oil and then began going through the drawers near the gas stove. He grabbed a book of matches and ran back to the stairs, squirting the oil all over the banisters and steps. He scraped a match against the edge of the box, but nothing happened. After a few more swipes of the match, a small fire sprang to life. He dropped the lit match into the pool of oil gathered at the bottom of the stairs. The fire spread quickly.

Biff smiled at Bill. "I always wanted to burn a house down."

Bill looked at him in astonishment, and then grabbed his arm. "Come on." They both ran out the door, Katie following them down the steps from the porch.

They kept running until Katie breathlessly called after them, "St-stop... can't go... any further."

They all stopped, trying to catch their breath, the smoke from the inn rising into the sky behind them.

"Oh Jesus... Oh God." Biff rubbed his forehead, fighting the oncoming hysteria. "Oh... God."

"Jesus..." Bill looked up to see the fountain filled with bones. "That's got to be everyone we know in there..." He turned and noticed what appeared to be a fleshy balloon floating next to him. He heard something like a chainsaw and felt a grinding pain in his chest. He stood in shock a moment, then cried out as he felt the buzzsaw exit his back.

Biff and Katie looked up as blood sprayed across the snow. A large floating creature was levitating next to Bill, a tail extending below it with a buzzsaw at its tip, now sticking out of Bill's back. It retracted its tail and flew up out of sight. Bill stood a moment longer, then his body slumped limply to the ground.

They both stared in silence a moment, then they heard a saw start up again and Biff turned to see one of the balloons coming at Katie, its blade cutting into her shoulder.

"No!" Biff cried, swinging the sledgehammer and knocking the thing to the ground. It let out a startled gasp, sounding as though it was struggling to breathe. Biff pounded the sledgehammer against its head. Again. And again. "No!" He was crying when Katie touched his shoulder and he dropped the sledgehammer, looking up at the sky where the thing that had killed Bill had been, now gone. "You killed my brother, you bastard!" he yelled up at the sky, falling to his knees and beginning to sob uncontrollably. "You killed him!"

Chapter 10

The boat sat frozen in place next to the small house. Nate and Nigel exited the man-made tunnel that led down the slope to the caretaker's house.

"Owen!" Nate called. He heard something fall into the snow behind him and turned to see a lumbering green monster seeping green slime coming toward them. "I am so sick of all these damn monsters!" Nate pumped the shotgun and blasted the thing right in the head. It fell to the ground, leaking more green pus everywhere. Nate turned back to Nigel. "Let's carry on, shall we-"

There was a green flash and something hit Nate across the face, knocking him off the dock and onto the frozen lake. The thing stood taller, raising its long arms above its head and sucking up the green substance it had leaked. It jumped off the dock and the ice began to crack as it lumbered toward Nate. He tried to stand, but kept slipping. The ice creaked and groaned under their weight. Nate threw the shotgun toward an area where the snow sloped to meet the ice to lessen his weight. When the gun landed, it went off, letting out a loud bang. The thing cried out, startled, and threw its long arms up in the air before slamming them down hard on the ice. A large crack cut through the ice and Nate fell through, along with the creature.

"Nate!" Nigel cried, but stopped when he stepped on the creaking ice.

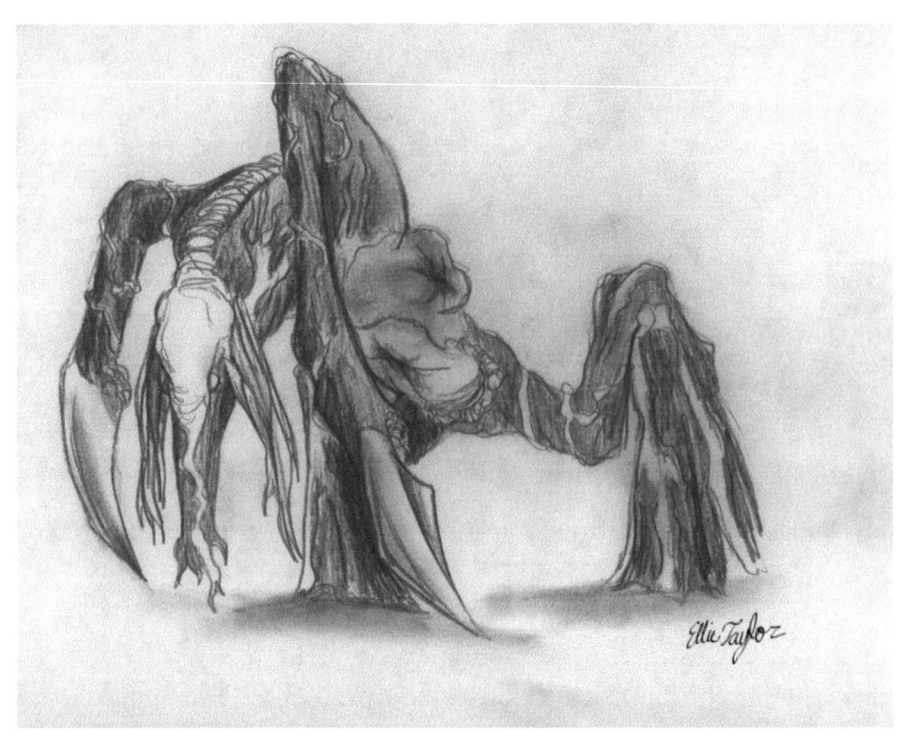

Nate opened his eyes even though the cold water stung them. He could see the monster sinking, unable to swim, and the hull of Owen's boat. He tried to kick his legs, to propel himself upward with his arms, but the shock of the sudden wet cold prevented him from moving.

He continued to watch the monster sink into the darkness below and he knew he was going to die. After surviving Bright Dawn and making it through Pelf to this boathouse, after seeing all of the lives it had claimed, he was going to drown and freeze and sink where no fishing net would ever bring up his remains. He felt anger welling up inside him. He had survived that thing that had killed Reese and Mary, but he was going to drown…

He was suddenly jerked up quickly by his coat collar and he could feel smooth ice against his back as he was dragged up the snowy slope. He felt someone begin to pound on his chest.

"Come on… Come on!" The voice sounded distant. "Come on, dammit! Don't you dare die on me Nate Grimfield!"

Nate coughed, feeling the icy water explode from his lungs. It reminded him of when Mary had coughed up all of that blood. He opened his eyes, but the wind stung them, so he closed them again.

"Goddammit, I think he's alive!" He heard the voice cry out joyfully; it was familiar. He heard the tone change, "You shut the hell up and find a way into that house! He'll catch hypothermia in these clothes."

Nate opened his eyes again. The sky was dark, but the snow was blindingly bright. He could make out the shape of a man stooped over him, but not the face. He coughed again and squinted his eyes, trying to focus. A face began to appear, fuzzy at first, but then Nate could see who it was clearly. His eyes widened and he tried to speak, but choked on what little water was still in his system. He rolled over on his side and spit it out, then looked back up at the figure.

"Dean…" he sounded breathless, gulping in the cold air; it burned his throat and lungs.

"Come on, get up, we need to get you dry clothes." Dean put Nate's arm over his shoulders and pulled him into the standing position. Nate's joints were stiff and he could feel the water droplets in his stubble freezing.

Nigel held the door to Owen's house open, walking in after them. "Nate, I am so sorry, the ice, it-"

"Shut up," Dean frowned with distaste at Nigel. "You were gonna let him drown... Find dry clothes." Nigel started to say something. "Do it!"

Nigel went to the closet and began looking through the clothes. "Don't give him such a hard time," Nate coughed.

"He was just standing there when I came outta the tunnel doing nothing, looking helpless. He was like that when he worked in the North Wing too; nervous and helpless."

"You may not like him, but he hasn't left me since all this started."

Nigel walked over with a flannel shirt, some black jeans, and a yellow fisherman jacket. "Sorry they're so big; Owen apparently was a big guy... I'll find some socks and underwear." He turned to go, "And Nate, the ice was cracking, I didn't know what to do, but I knew I wouldn't be any good to you if I fell through too."

Nate saw Dean stop himself from saying something unpleasant. "I understand Nigel." Dean began to peel the wet clothes off Nate. "And where the hell have you been?" Nate demanded.

"Trapped." Dean slapped the wet lab coat onto the floor, "Then hiding. Richardson found out I'd been in the West Wing." He turned and yelled over his shoulder, "And I need a towel!" then turned back to Nate, "And he locked me up. The guy's a loon, something is seriously wrong with him. He was experimenting on all those people in there. And you shoulda seen those bastards like the one that crawled through your vent. Nasty little… *slug* things!" Nigel handed him a towel and he draped it around Nate's shoulders. He grabbed Nate's coat and began through the pockets. He pulled out the pistol and shotgun shells. "Great… Ruined." He reached into the other pocket and pulled out the matted Paradise postcards. "Hey, you've got some of these too?"

"Yeah," Nate pulled the towel tighter around himself, "signed 'William.'"

"Redmoor?"

"I'm guessing."

Dean tried to read them, but the ink was all blotched and undecipherable. "What'd yours say?"

"'For God's sake, get out before it's too late.' and 'It's spreading like cancer. Hurry!'"

"I can't find any shoes," Nigel dropped the socks and underwear on the pile of dry clothes.

"I'll let you change," Dean stood and turned his back. "My postcards said 'I was just the beginning. He's already started Phase Two. Things are going to get much worse.' and right before I found you, I found one that read 'Too late for escape now. You must go back to the prison and stop him.'" He tilted his head, "Odd that he would write that since it's not a prison anymore…"

"So how did you find us anyway?" Nate pulled on the dry pants.

"I was looking for survivors and a way out when I saw your tracks in the snow. What are you doing all the way out here?"

"Looking for Owen Rice, the lighthouse caretaker who went missing. This is his house and boat- oh shit!"

"What?"

"I left the damn key to the boat back in my room at Bright Dawn!" Nate exclaimed.

"You mean this?" Nate turned as Dean retrieved a key from his pocket. It dangled from a nautical keychain.

"Yes! But how?…"

"When I got out, I went to find you. When you weren't in your room, I saw this sitting on your desk and just kinda grabbed it… Thought it might come in handy." Nate took the key and began for the door. "Whoa," Dean grabbed him, "we gotta find you some dry shoes."

"There aren't any shoes," Nigel restated.

They all stood a moment, then Dean walked across the room and pulled some books off of the shelf, throwing them on the floor. He then took a lighter from one of the many pockets on his jacket.

"And another thing," he said, lighting the books on fire, "you can only kill those green ones with fire." Dean set Nate's shoes by the fire, hoping the heat would warm and dry them.

"You been to the metal room?" Nate asked, sitting close to the fire, "With the green sky."

"Yeah… twice. Don't really know how I got there or how I got out… Just kinda happened."

"We went there once - at the lighthouse."

"Weird stuff." Dean walked across the room and Nate noticed the pile of guns in the corner for the first time. He saw Mosher's shotgun, but he also saw a machine gun and what appeared to be a sniper rifle. Dean strapped the sniper rifle across his back and draped the machine gun strap over his shoulder so he could easily grab and fire it. He brought Nate the shotgun. "Those shoes dry yet?"

~~~~~~~~~~~~~~~~~~~~~~~~~~~

Dean, Nate, and Nigel exited Owen's house and walked onto the boat's deck. It was a decently sizable craft, with one door leading to its interior. Nate tried the door, but it was locked. He looked at Nigel and Dean before unlocking the door and opening it. The ice on the windows was so thick that only a small amount of light leaked in. Nigel turned on the flashlight and shined it around the inside of the cabin. Next to them was a table with a wraparound booth and small kitchenette. They continued to the front of the boat where they could see the steering controls and a chair.

And there hung Owen Rice, strung up by his feet, his arms tied behind his back. There were deep rips in his chest, red icicles hanging from his body where his blood had frozen. The cabinet below him was open, containing a small box with an electric bolt sticker on its side. The elevator battery. Nate got down on his hands and knees to retrieve it, trying to avoid the red ice slick below Owen.

As Nate grabbed the battery, he looked up at Owen's frostbitten face. Owen, who had welcomed him to Pelf. Owen, the outsider. Owen, who had laughed at the Pratchett brothers and their friendly ways. This could not be what he deserved.

He grasped the battery in his hands and turned to his friends. "He's been here the whole time…" He stood, still clutching the battery. "I…" He was scared, but his fear was quickly turning into anger, "I wanna know what was down there… I wanna get whatever did this to him!" he pointed at Owen's frozen corpse.

Nigel looked uncertain, but Dean stepped forward. "I'm in."

Nigel sighed, pinching the bridge of his nose. "Okay."

They began through the tunnel back up the slope toward the lighthouse and Pelf. Nate pulled Owen's fisherman jacket tighter around himself - it was at least two or three sizes too large for him.

"Killed plenty of them," Dean remarked as they passed the half-buried tick creature.

They entered the mine and Dean began toward the shed. "Dean, the elevator." But Dean was not listening, he was already shining his light around inside the shed.

"Just a lot of boxes." He kicked the door open and ventured inside. He shined his light into the nearest box, "Dynamite…" Nigel connected the cables to the battery and the elevator roared to life, causing both of them to jump. "It's *full* of dynamite," Dean walked out of the shed as Nate was climbing onto the elevator. "We need somebody to stand watch." Dean looked at Nigel, who made no move to argue. He climbed onto the elevator, grabbing ahold of his machine gun and giving Nate a reassuring smile. Nate pulled the lever and they began the journey down. The elevator was slow-moving and whirred loudly; Nate wondered how safe it was to be riding this thing. When they reached the bottom, Nate shined the flashlight around. It was a large tunnel, with frozen metal tracks that had at one time housed mining cars that were now lying on their sides by the wall.

Dean took a step forward. "Well-" he started, but everything went green and the rock walls became a greasy chrome, stained red by blood. Where the tunnel had extended before them now stood a large building that resembled Bright Dawn, but looked decades older. The ground began to shake and a large, bloody blade erupted from the roof of the prison. As the walls of the building collapsed and fell away, a monstrosity was revealed. It held another equally large blade in its other hand, each about the size of a city bus. Its skin was beginning to decay in places, and its nose had completely rotted away. It had two black holes where its eyes should have been. It roared, the force knocking Nate and Dean down. It grimaced down at them, its rotted teeth clenched. It looked like a much larger zombie, only without the gaping chest cavity.

Dean stood and pulled the trigger, raining bullets all across its soft belly, but they bounced off, causing no damage whatsoever. It looked at them, gurgling angrily.

"Oh shit!" Dean yelled and they both turned, running for the metal shaft that had once been the elevator. Nate silently rejoiced that the control panel had remained mostly the same. He threw the lever and they began up, but the Colossus was advancing quickly. It slammed one of its blades against the shaft just below the lift and they grabbed the rails on the sides for support. It roared loudly, throwing its head back in rage.

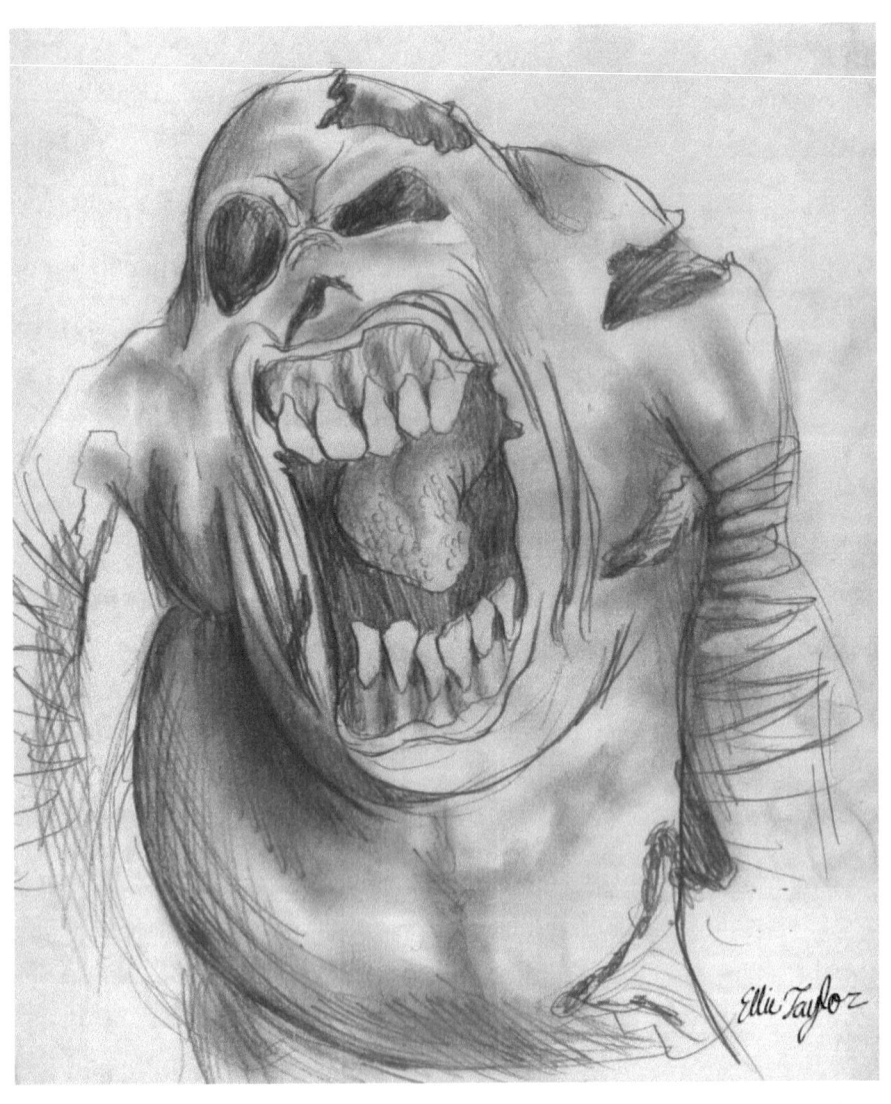

"Oh no! It's happening again!" they could hear Nigel screaming above them. When they reached the top, they both ran off the lift. "What's down there?" Nigel asked desperately. "I heard explosions."

"Explosions…" Dean said to himself and Nigel looked over the edge into the face of the Colossus. He gasped and began to fall sideways, fainting, but Dean caught him by the shoulder and slapped him across the face. "Snap out of it and follow me!"

Nigel put his hand to his stinging cheek, but followed Dean to the metal building, Nate close behind. Dean threw open the door and to reveal a room full of wooden crates. He reached into one, pulling out a stick of dynamite.

"It didn't change…" he said, astonished but relieved. "… Here! Get these to the lift!" He slid the stick of dynamite into his breast pocket and handed a crate to Nigel and one to Nate. He lifted two and began across the room. The floor shook, no doubt from the Colossus trying to reach them. It roared again, sending a strange vibration throughout the room.

The weight of the crates was too much and Dean's knees gave out, and he fell to the ground. Nate ran back to him. "What were you thinking!?" He lifted one of the crates.

"Chaplain Kennedy believed in us, Nate… I think he knew something like this was coming." Dean tried to catch his breath, "Why else would he have told us about the prison and those men who died in the mines? He *chose* us… We can't let him down!"

Nate had not thought about the Chaplain since they had escaped Bright Dawn. "Come on," he stood with the crate, "let's get this thing."

Dean grabbed the remaining crate and they ran to the lift, setting them beside the other two. Dean pulled the lever and leapt back to the land where Nigel and Nate stood. As the lift descended, he pulled the stick of dynamite from his pocket and lit the end before dropping it after the lift. They heard the first explosion, followed by a series of explosions. The fire began to come up the shaft and the three backed up quickly. But suddenly they were back in the coal mine, still pushed backwards by what little force of the explosion had made it through.

Nate turned to Dean, "Have you seen Kennedy?"

"No… You two are the first living people I've seen since I escaped."

"We have to go back… He might still be alive!" Nate stood. "He'll know what to do."

"Wait," Nigel also stood, "you wanna go back there?"

"It's not like we're any safer out here," Nate stated matter-of-factly.

"He's right," Dean gripped the machine gun. "We don't have any choice but to go back… or freeze out here." He pulled the postcard out of his pocket, "'Too late for escape now. You must go back to the prison and stop him.'"

"We're basing this decision off of what Redmoor said!?" Nigel exclaimed hysterically. Nate and Dean looked at him seriously. What other choice did they have?

Chapter 11

The inn came into view, black and charred against the white snow. The smell of smoke was still in the air. As they neared, Nate could see the door was smashed in. He ran up the porch, shining the light inside. "Hello? Hoover?" A hand shot up and grabbed his arm, causing him to scream. He hit its fingers with the butt of his gun, then shined the flashlight down at its body. A zombie lay under some rubble where the roof had collapsed, looking defeated yet still vicious.

Nate descended the steps. "Nobody in there."

As the fountain of bones came into view, so did a red lump partially buried in the snow. Dean ran ahead, his gun poised. He nudged the lump with his foot, rolling it over. The face of a young man came into view, blood dried around his nose and mouth. There was a large bloody rip through his chest.

"It's a body," he called back as Nate and Nigel approached, Nigel slightly more hesitant then Nate.

Nate froze when he saw the face. "Bill." He looked around, but did not see any footprints in the snow. "Biff!" he yelled. "Katie!" No answer besides the howling wind. "Biff!" The door to Mosher's creaked open and they all turned, their guns aimed at the door.

"In here," Biff's voice sounded strained. "We're in here. Get inside before it gets you too!"

The three jogged over to Mosher's and got inside. "What do you mean 'it'?" Nigel asked.

"It… it came outta the sky… and it just killed him." Biff looked over at Katie who was sitting on the floor, her arms wrapped around her knees. "Just cut right through him…"

"But *what* was it?" Dean asked impatiently.

Biff shrugged and slowly shook his head. "I… I don't know. It was just a big thing that came outta the sky and had a freakin' buzzsaw coming out of its ass that it drove through my brother's chest. Coming out of its ass, man!" He raised his voice, then said more quietly, "And those other things got Vincent Hoover… Didn't get to rip him up though, he had a heart attack first."

Nate looked over at Katie, who had yet to say a word.

"We've gotta get outta here before it does," Dean looked around at everyone. "We need to warn people."

"How? We can't get out," Biff said.

"We have to find a way," Dean replied sternly. "We can try to find a way through Bright Dawn; you try to find a way through Pelf," he nodded toward Biff. "But we have to get out. If we find a way through Bright Dawn, we'll pick you up in one of the cars. If you get out, you can…" He looked between Biff and Katie.

"Vincent had a truck… He kept it parked outside the village gate," Katie spoke for the first time. "I have the keys."

"All right," Dean looked back to Nate and Nigel, "we can do this… Who's with me?"

Biff looked down at Katie, then lifted the sledgehammer, resting it on his shoulder. "We'll get out."

"We'll go back and find the Chaplain; he will know what to do," Dean sighed. Nate nodded in agreement. Nigel no longer seemed to have much resolve in him. "Come on," Dean motioned toward the tunnel in the closet.

Katie jumped up and wrapped her arms around Nate's neck. "Don't die in there," she whispered in his ear.

"We'll see you and Biff when we get out," he said decisively. She pulled back and he forced a smile. She held back tears and kissed his damaged cheek before letting him go.

~~~~~~~~~~~~~~~~~~~~~~~~~~

Dean exited the tunnel first, aiming his gun around the boiler room. Nate came next, followed by Nigel. They entered the basement hallway and the speakers of the intercom system sprang to life. They all stopped, ducking and looking around wildly.

"How can those be working if the power's out?" Nigel gasped.

"I knew you'd come back," the Doctor's voice came over the speakers. "Welcome to Bright Dawn Medical Treatment Center." There was a pause. "You appear to have injured my pet... He did not take too kindly to that. But then again, neither did I." They could hear something making its way along the corridor. "Time for surgery." The creature that had killed Reese and Mary rounded the corner, blood caked on one side of its massive head. It spotted them and roared angrily. "Good-bye," the intercom shut off. It cried out angrily again and began running down the hall, gradually gaining speed. Dean loaded a new clip into the machine gun and raised it, opening fire on the creature. It roared in pain, but kept coming.

"Run!" Dean yelled, beginning back down the hallway. Bullets stopped coming out of the gun and it was upon him. He hit it across the face with the empty gun. It screeched, retaliating by knocking him to the ground. It raised one clawed hand and brought it down, catching Dean's jacket, pinning him to the floor. He quickly reloaded the gun as it tried to get its claw unstuck from his bullet-proof jacket. He fired and bullets exploded from the top of its head. Its claw came loose and it stumbled backwards like a drunk, roaring weakly, then fell on its side, breathing in quick, shallow gasps.

Dean walked over to it. "G'night, Fido," he said, emptying the rest of the clip into its head. He turned to the security camera and walked right up to it, able to see his reflection in the lens. "Even though the power's not on, I know you can hear me and I know you can see me. I'm gonna stop you - *we're* gonna stop you. You hear me, you bastard. I'm gonna do to you what I did to your pet." He flipped off the camera before busting in the lens, and then turned back to the other two. "I say we pay the good Doctor a visit."

Dean led the way onto the second floor, his gun aimed down the hallway. "The security storage room isn't too far from here. There should be plenty of ammo left in there." The airshaft creaked above them and he aimed his gun up at the ceiling. "And watch the vents."

Dean opened the door and stepped inside the storage room. There were cabinets and drawers of ammunition, gun cabinets, and spare uniforms hanging in a row. As Dean began to go through the cabinets, Nate shrugged off Owen's jacket and began to look for a uniform closer to his size. He located a navy button down shirt and cargo pants.

"Dammit," Dean looked inside the gun cabinet. "Empty… Guess we'll just have to make do with what we have." He returned to the ammunition cabinets and retrieved boxes of shotgun shells, machine gun magazines, and pistol clips. Dean clipped the ammunition to his belt and Nigel slid his into his coat pockets, "Here," Dean offered Nate a belt somewhat like his own and he slipped the shot gun shells into one of his new pants pockets.

As they stepped outside of the storage room, the metal grate of a ceiling vent fell in front of them, narrowly missing Dean's head. Nigel and Dean both aimed their lights up at the empty hole in the ceiling. Blood began to drip down, splattering on the floor loudly in the silence. Then they heard a sound from inside the shaft, like the beginning of a cry.

Dean's eyes widened, "Run!"

Nigel did not need to be told twice. He was running down the hall toward the stairs but Nate continued to stare up at the vent. He was rooted to the spot by a sick and dangerous curiosity; a curiosity to see what had been crawling over him that night as he slept. When had that been? That night felt years away now as he stood in the dark hallway. A mauve and green blob fell from the hole. Dean was backing away from it, keeping his light trained on it. His description had not been too far off; it looked like a slug, about the size of a cat. It opened its mouth, exposing several rows of razor sharp teeth and the cry it let out sounded like that of a human infant. He heard the shaft creaking above him - there were more. Finally his feet came unglued and he turned, running, Dean not far behind him, infantile crying filling the air.

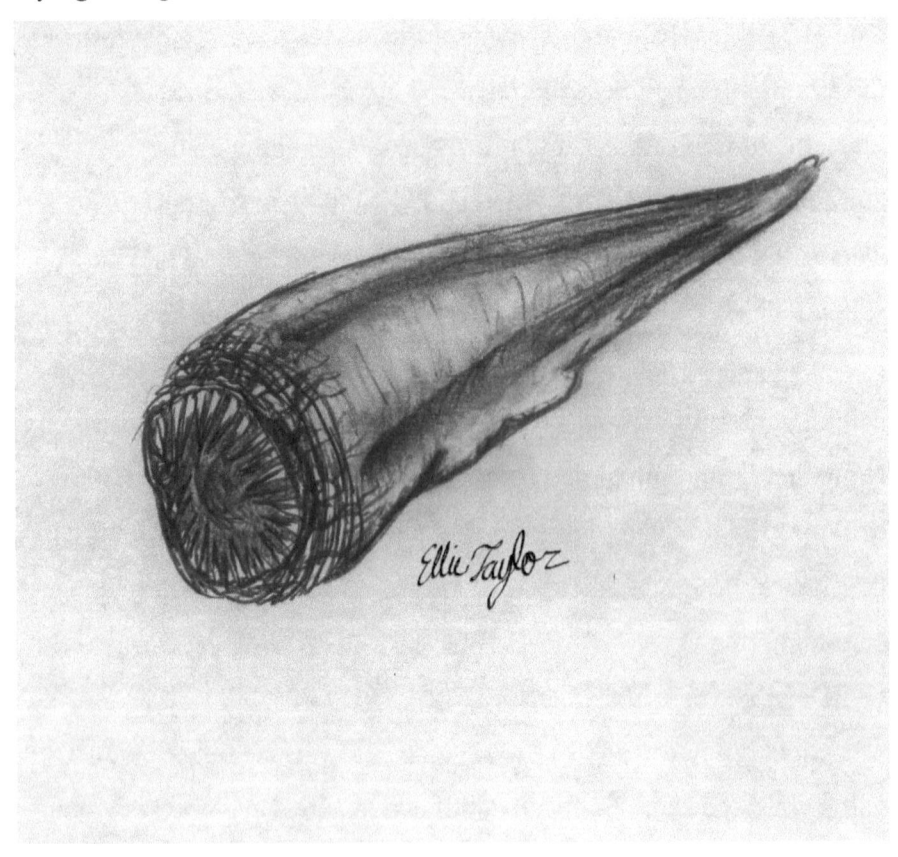

"Hurry!" Nigel had his hand on the door, ready to close it once Nate and Dean were through. They were fast, the first had nearly caught up to Dean as they ran through the door and Nigel pushed it closed. There was a sickening crack and the cry became gurgled. Nigel looked down to see he had caught the thing in the door, nearly cutting it in half. Dark blood was shooting out of its mouth. His arm turned to jelly and the door began to open.

"No!" Dean grabbed it, kicking the slug out of the way and pushing the door closed. "We can't let them get in here!"

The door jolted and Nate could hear them crying on the other side. There had to be at least four or five of them. Dean pushed his whole weight against the door.

"Get something heavy to put against it." The door jolted again, knocking Dean to the ground. "Do it!" Despite the cold, sweat was running down Dean's face.

They were so small, how could they be so strong? Nate saw Nigel frantically searching for something to put against the door. They heard someone begin to cry a floor above them. "Hey!" Nigel yelled out, running up the stairs. "We're coming, hold on!" He crested the last step and turned to see the floating head of an old man crying pitifully. He froze and it inhaled deeply, then spit in his direction. He saw something moving behind the head as he put his arm up to shield his face. Black ink stained his sleeve as Nate reached the top of the stairs. He saw the head and remembered he had left his shotgun down with Dean.

"*What an idiot!*" he mentally yelled at himself. He grabbed Nigel's pistol and shot the head between the eyes. It cried out as more black gunk spewed out of the hole in its head before deflating and sinking down. Something moved in the shadows and an angry scream erupted as a new terrifying face emerged.

It looked down at its fallen partner, then back at the two men, its huge yellow eyes shifting between them.

"Guys, come on! I can't hold this much longer!" Dean yelled breathlessly from below.

Nate raised the gun and shot, but nothing happened, just a dull click. He looked at the gun in his hand, tears welling up in his eyes. "It's empty…"

The thing let out a scream and lunged forward. Nate lost his footing and began to tumble down the stairs. Nigel stood frozen, unarmed, not knowing where to go as the spear that was its tongue flew at his face.

---- End Part 2 ----

Part 3: The Plane of Anguish

Chapter 12

Nate caught the banister and looked up in time to see Nigel move out of the head's way as it crashed into the wall. Its tongue retracted, leaving a decently sized hole in the wall.

"Too... strong," Dean grunted through gritted teeth. "Hurry up!"

The head turned to Nigel, glaring and baring its teeth. Nigel looked over his shoulder to see a glass case framed by red and white stripes. Inside was a fire ax. He hesitated before breaking the glass in with his elbow, then remembered the alarm would not go off since the power was out and smashed the glass. The head screeched and lunged once more; Nigel cut his hand reaching through the broken window to grab the ax. He swung, catching the creature in the mouth with the handle. It recoiled, then lunged again. This time the blade came in contact with its mouth. As it froze, astonished, not knowing what to do, Nigel brought the ax down on its tongue, severing it from the creature's face. His knees gave out and he fell to the ground. He could feel his heart rate going up at a dangerous rate and sweat forming on his half-frozen forehead. He closed his eyes, trying to take deep breaths and think of somewhere - *anywhere* - better than here. He could not afford a panic attack now; none of them could.

The crying below grew louder for a moment, then they heard Dean groan and the door slam back closed. "Holy shit!... Are you guys alive up there?"

Nate pulled himself up along the stairs by the banister and slowed as he passed Nigel - who appeared to be in a trance - but kept going.

He turned into the first office he saw and began looking around for something heavy. He saw a loaded file cabinet in the corner. It looked sturdy, tan finish over metal, and if it was full it would be nearly impossible to move. He had to try. He grabbed the next to top handle and pulled. It scooted, but not very far. He tugged again. Once again, a small shift. His arms ached, but he pulled again. It moved farther this time; it almost felt lighter. He looked up to see Nigel had slid in behind it and was pushing.

"Come on, pull… I can't push this by myself."

Nate gripped the handle and pulled, and the two moved the file cabinet to the stairs.

"We're gonna have to carry it down." Nate tipped it over on its side and grabbed one of the handles. As they lifted it, Nigel cried out, the cuts on his shoulders reopening and new bright blood running down his arms.

"I can't do it, man." He let go of the cabinet, "I just can't."

Nate sat down his end and walked to Nigel's. He looked around a moment, then put the ball of his foot against the top of the cabinet, gripping the banisters on either side, and gave it a hard kick. It tumbled down the stairs, hitting the wall with a loud crash.

"Oh fuck me!" Dean cried out, exasperated. "That better be one of you!"

"Coming down!" Nate descended the stairs, Nigel close behind. Nate and Nigel both got behind the file cabinet. "Push!" They slid it along the floor toward the door. Dean watched until they nearly ran it into his calves before moving. They all three stood back, staring at the door. The slugs continued to pound against the door, but the cabinet did not budge.

"Oh Jesus," Dean leaned against the wall, sliding down into the sitting position. "I gotta catch my breath... Damn, my knees hurt!" He looked up at them. "What the hell took you two so long?"

"There were more... 'friends' upstairs," Nate scratched his unshaven chin.

"More slugs?"

"No... flying heads." Dean's eyes widened. "There were two... One spit ink and the other had a spear thing for a tongue. We only encountered two, but there may be more."

"Damn," Dean leaned his head back against the wall.

~~~~~~~~~~~~~~~~~~~~~~~~~~~

Biff brought the sledgehammer down on the gate again. His arms ached and he had barely made any headway. He rested the sledgehammer on the ground, leaning on the handle. After a bit, he lifted the sledgehammer again, but Katie grabbed his arm.

"Biff, look," she said quietly, pointing out toward the lake. Thick green clouds were approaching fast.

Biff lowered the sledgehammer. "We need to get inside," he said, staring at the approaching clouds.

They began toward Mosher's, the nearest building. Biff slowed as they passed the lump of red snow that was Bill's body, then continued on. Once inside, Biff locked the door and turned to see Katie with her arms wrapped around herself, shivering. He frantically began rummaging through the shelves and bins to find something to

155

warm the place up. He opened a cabinet and found a portable gas stove, a small canister of propane behind it. He brought the chair laying in the center of the room to where Katie sat on the ground.

"Just hold on," he said absently, setting the stove up on the chair. "I'll get you warm."

Little blue flames came up from the burners and he sat beside her, opening up his jacket and pulling her inside, rubbing her arms to warm her up. She put her hands inside his coat, hugging him. He could feel how cold her hands were through his shirt.

"I'm sorry," she looked up at him as he spoke. "I'm sorry I couldn't save Bill... I... I know how you felt about him."

"What happened wasn't your fault... He was your brother too... I loved him," she sniffed, "but I wasn't in love with him... He was my best friend."

He sighed, looking up at the ceiling. "Oh, who then? Dr. Grimfield?" He looked back at her.

She shook her head and laughed sadly. "No... I don't see why you're so blind," her eyes met his. "I love *you* Biff."

He felt his eyes swell with tears. "What?"

"I've loved you forever, but you were always too busy trying to outdo Bill and impress me that you never saw it. I wanted you to make a move... But you never would and when Bill did, I decided to give it a try. But it just wasn't the same... I think he knew that." Biff hugged her closer to him as her voice cracked. "He said that us being together was hurting you and he just couldn't do it..."

He held her close, trying not to cry. His brother - his wonderful brother - had given up what he loved for him; he had carried Katie down the stairs and come back for him. He had knocked that thing to the ground right before it would have had him. As if it was not enough that he had ripped his own heart out for his brother, that monster had come from the sky and scattered it all across the snow. Bill had always been the better man, yet Biff was still alive and Bill lay cold and dead in the snow.

Katie leaned her head against his shoulder. "Biff," she whispered, "don't get killed trying to protect me... I can manage." Her breathing grew heavy and he knew she was asleep.

~~~~~~~~~~~~~~~~~~~~~~~~~~~~

Dean stopped when they reached the door labeled '6.' "Okay," he whispered, "who knows what he's got guarding his office. I'm gonna go through first." He gripped the machine gun, and then went through the door. He froze. The hall was completely silent... too quiet. It was eerie. Dean hesitated for a moment outside Dr. Richardson's office before opening the door. He aimed the gun around the room, but it was as still and quiet as the hall. "Come on," he whispered to the other two and once they had entered the office, he closed the door behind them. The office seemed to have been untouched by the manifestation; the desk was still neat, all of the chairs upright, no blood stains on the carpet.

A sheet had been draped over something on the far side of the room. Dean lifted it to reveal a mirror, then let the sheet fall over it once more. Nate stepped forward and heard something crunch under his shoe. He looked down at his feet to see the Doctor's stereo and CDs had been shattered and now lay spread across the floor. Dean had found his way to the desk and was shining his flashlight across the Doctor's papers.

A ledger lay open on the desk. Dean read aloud, "Malatesta reaches into the real world, psychoplasmic eruption — good God, William! — infects host... me! Tries to open path between two planes. MUST STOP, must get her out of my head!... cannot stop... must open pathway." He looked up, "What is 'Malatesta?'" Dean lifted the ledger to find another book underneath it, a red ribbon bookmark sticking out from between two pages. Dean turned to the page and read, "Malatesta: an ancient serpent trapped in the lowest Plane of Anguish. Centuries spent within the Plane have twisted this creature into a demented, rage-filled beast of immense power. Malatesta can only be harmed in the deepest reaches of Anguish. If it breaks free of this realm, it becomes invincible..." He flipped through the pages. "Wonder where this book came from..." He noticed another page with the corner folded down. He turned to it and read, "Some believe the Plane to be just a myth used to explain feelings of grief. Others believe to reach it, you must first go through immense pain: both psychically and physically. The opening of such a gateway could result in the annihilation of life as we know it. The dead would rule the living..."

Nate knelt to examine the broken pieces of the Doctor's CDs. A pattern began to emerge and when he tilted his head slightly to the left, he could see that they made out capital letters: D. E. A. D. The fragments spelled out 'DEAD.'

"No trace of Richardson." Nigel exchanged which hand held his pistol.

"Why would he have marked these pages in this book?" Dean snapped the book closed and opened the main drawer of the Doctor's desk. "Well I'll be-" he pulled out an old newspaper. "This is an article about that prisoner riot." He picked up another newer-looking article. "'Pclf Mines Close After Tragic Accident.'" He frowned at the next object, "An empty clipboard…"

"Let me see that," Nate took it from him. "This is my old clipboard." He recognized the symbol carved into the lower corner, faded ink next to it reading, 'What is William trying to say?'

The intercom sprang to life, "Good job, boys, you found my secret book. Too bad you won't be able to share. You have greatly inconvenienced me. But no matter, cut off one head and I will grow two more in its place." The office fell silent.

"We have to find Kennedy, see if he's still alive," Nate said quietly.

"He has to be!" Nigel exclaimed hysterically. "He's our only hope."

Gunfire broke out below them, accompanied by a guttural roar and someone yelling. "You like that you big bastard? Come get some more!"

159

Chapter 13

Dean raced to the door, his gun at the ready. He opened the door to the still, empty hallway and began down the stairs. The gunshots continued, from the sound of it another machine gun like Dean's. Nate followed with the shotgun, but Nigel picked up the book Dean had been reading and turned to the first page. "The Plane of Anguish exists in the depths of our being. It is believed to be a place devoid of all joy and life. One philosopher described it as 'a world where the dead walk, trapped within metal prison walls, under a sky that never ceases to be cloudy.' The color green is often associated with the Plane…"

As Dean exited the stairwell, he turned to see a man flung through one of the windows to Surgery Room E. He hit the wall with a loud thud and crumpled to the ground. A roar that shook the walls came from within the surgery room. The floor shook as whatever was in there took a step forward. The slumped figure moved, raising his gun one last time and holding down the trigger. A pitiful cry came from the room, and then the whole floor shook, causing Nate and Dean to nearly lose their balance.

A large appendage studded with spikes and wrapped in barbed wire could be seen sticking out of the doorway in a spreading pool of blood. The man slumped over once more, limp and still. Dean slowly approached him, rolling him over to reveal his face. The eyes were glassy and stared off blankly, some blood trickling out of his partially parted lips.

"I know him," Dean said quietly as Nate approached. "Carlos Frewer, he was one of the guards in the North Wing with me... He stopped who guy that stabbed you from holding onto that shank." Nate vaguely remembered a guard taking the crazy man by the wrist as Dean had dragged him away. Dean turned his flashlight to the creature that lay in surgery.

"... All of the inhabitants in the Plane are believed to be warped and demented in some fashion, but none so much as Malatesta: an ancient serpent trapped in the lowest Plane of Anguish," Nigel had reached the page with the red bookmark.

The creature was large, at least two times the size of the thing that had killed Mary. It had several large incisions cut into its body, stitched closed, red and pus-filled. Its mouth housed jagged teeth with no lips to cover them and two large clubs for arms, studded with spikes and wrapped in barbed wire up to the shoulder. It was a miserable-looking creature.

"Dear God…" Nate whispered as Nigel ran down the stairs.

"I know where we've been," Nigel said, out of breath. "We have been to that place, in Richardson's book. It's described as a metal prison, where cloud cover never lets up. The color green is also highly associated with it. The green clouds…" he looked between them. "And that-that's where these things co-come from." He stopped, forcing himself to take a few deep breaths. "And that's why some of them don't seem even remotely human." His eyes widened and his voice grew hoarse, "They're from another world."

~ ~

Biff awoke, shivering slightly, and when he looked down at his arm he saw a small layer of frost forming on his jacket sleeve. He looked up to see no more blue flames coming from the stove. They had run out of propane.

"No," he stood, still disoriented, waking Katie. He stared at the flameless burners for a moment longer before switching it to 'off' and detaching the empty canister.

"It's so cold." Biff did not hear her as he walked to the window and wiped a small circle with his sleeve. He peered out. More of the zombies they had encountered at the inn filled the foggy streets. Across the village square he could see a tank of propane on an abandoned porch. He knew he had to get it. Without it, he and Katie would freeze to death.

He zipped up his coat and turned to Katie. "I'm going out there."

"No!" She gripped his arm, her eyes wide with fear.

"I have to. *Heat* is out there," he brushed a strand of hair out of her face, smiling reassuringly. "I used to run in football, back in high school, remember? I've still got it." He placed the nail gun in her hand. "I just need you to cover me."

He gripped the door handle, taking a deep breath. He pulled the door open, bolting across the snow. All of the wandering zombies looked up as Biff ran up the steps of the porch. He grabbed the tank by its handle and swung it around, bashing one of the zombies in the head.

"Shoot, Katie!" he shouted, heading back toward the general store. She began firing, hitting some zombies, their hearts exploding, missing others. Biff leapt to avoid tripping over a fallen zombie when he felt a sharp pain in his shoulder and heard Katie scream. He tried to ignore the pain and nearly slipped when he landed, but regained his footing and kept going. Once inside, he slammed the door closed behind him and leaned against it, sliding down into a sitting position. He released the tank of propane.

"Oh God, Biff, I am so sorry!" He turned to see blood running out of his shoulder and a nail protruding from the wound.

He tried to speak in between his heavy breaths. "It's okay… We're safe now." He stood, turning the lock on the door and moving to the stove to attach the propane. After a moment, he spoke again. "I told you I could outrun them."

She walked over to him, shining the flashlight on his shoulder. "We should get this out before it gets infected."

"Will this scar make me more ruggedly handsome?" he joked, but she avoided his eyes. "Hey," he caught her arm, "it wasn't your fault; I'm fine." He reached up and gripped the nail between his fingers, pulling it out. He clenched his jaw to avoid screaming and then dropped the nail to the floor. "See, not a big deal."

"I… I thought when I shot you that you'd fall and… and… they'd get you." She began to cry.

Biff wiped away her tears. "No don-don't cry. I'm fine," he hugged her, trying to avoid getting blood on her sweater. "We're both fine."

"Do you think they got Nate and the others?"

"No," Biff shook his head, silently hoping that he was right.

~~~~~~~~~~~~~~~~~~~~~~~~~~~~~

"I'm sure if Kennedy's anywhere, he's holed up in his office." Dean shined his flashlight down at the bloody mess that had once been Reese Caulderstone. He shined the light back in front of him and it reflected off of a white coat. He yelled out, stopping abruptly, causing Nate to run into him.

"Don't-don't shoot!" Keith McDonnell held up his hands.

"W-w-what are you doing here?" Nigel's voice was higher than usual.

"You called me; you said there was a situation-"

"I told you not to come," Nigel pressed his palm against his forehead. "That call was a warning… It didn't all get through, but I'd hoped it was enough…"

"And what is going on?" Keith looked around. "One minute I was outside, and then I was in this odd metal chamber and I walked a few steps and then I was here."

"I don't know how to explain it…" Nate was as appalled as Nigel that Keith had arrived. He saw something move behind Keith and shot an approaching zombie right before it grabbed him.

"What the hell is that!?" Keith pointed down at the zombie, now scared. He whipped around as they all heard what sounded like whispering behind him. He squinted into the shadows and as he did so, the darkness seemed to shift, to inch closer to him. As it neared, the whispers grew more ominous and six orange eyes suddenly became visible. Keith was paralyzed and the shadow continued to advance. When it touched him, he disappeared.

"It… it ate him!" Nigel cried after a moment. "It just… ate him!"

"I don't know if it ate him, but we need to get out of here before another one of us disappears." Dean turned and ran toward the kitchen. Once they were inside, he barred the door, sliding his sniper rifle through the handles.

As Nate backed away from the door, a kitchen cabinet opened, and a man fell out. Tufts of blonde hair were growing out of his stitched head. He sat up, clutching his stomach with one hand and holding something in the other. His wide blue eyes met Nate's.

"William Redmoor," Nate said quietly in shocked recognition. His eyes drifted down to William's stomach. He had an awful-looking large burnt gash, green pus mixed with blood seeping out around his fingers. "Quick, get him up on the table!" He knocked some pots and pans off of a counter and Dean helped him lift him up onto it. "Nigel, see what you can find in the cabinets, a first aid kit maybe." He turned back to William. "William, can you hear me?" William nodded. "Did you leave these postcards?" He held up one of Dean's postcards from Paradise. William nodded. Nate lowered the postcard and went back to examining his festering abrasion.

"I didn't kill my wife," William choked out.

Nigel continued to rummage through cabinets but froze when he spotted a mirror over the sink.

"What?" Nate frowned, turning back to William's face.

"Find the priest." He lifted his other hand, "He knows. He knows about the Doctor."

"The priest? Chaplain Kennedy?" Dean asked eagerly.

"Which Doctor?" Nate asked.

William began to cry. "The one that touched my brain."

A face wrapped in black surgeon attire and goggles gazed back at Nigel from the mirror. "Nate…"

"Take this," William held out something to Nate. "It's the key." Nate looked down at William's hand and his blood ran cold. The item in William's hand looked like the carving from his clipboard. He slowly took it. "It's the key…"

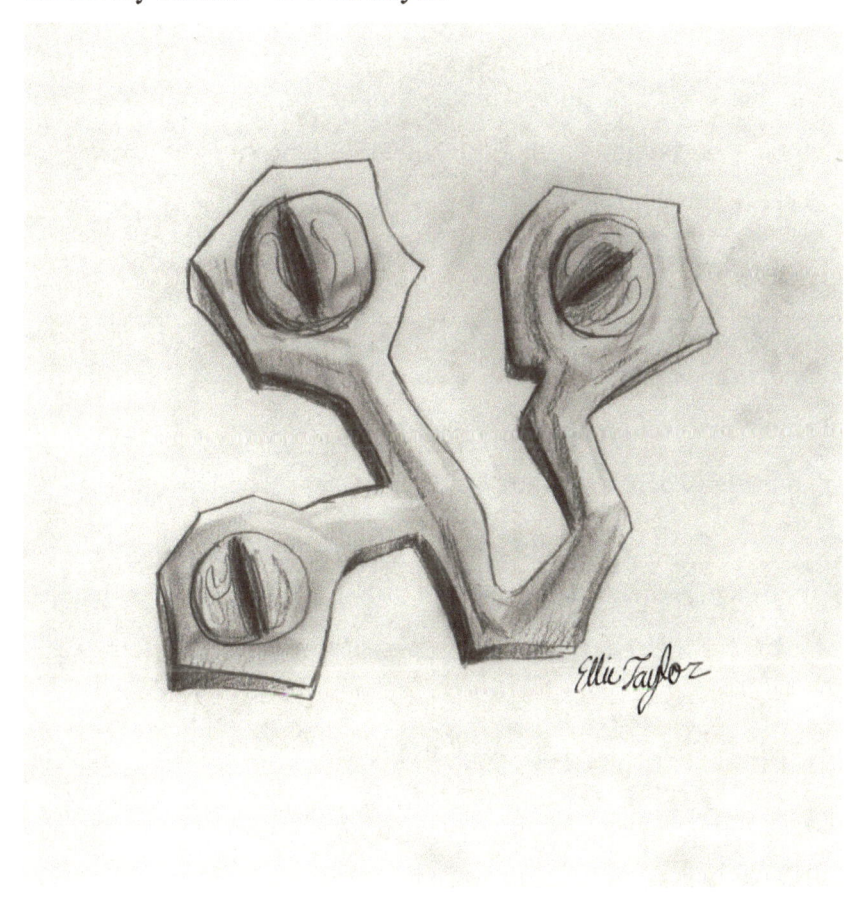

"Nate," Nigel turned from the mirror but one of the Doctor's black-gloved hands reached out, grabbing his hair. He tried to run, but the Doctor pulled him back by his head. "Nate!"

Nate turned as the Doctor's other arm emerged from the mirror. Something glinted in the dim light and he sunk the scalpel in his hand into Nigel's exposed throat.

"No!" Nate cried out as Richardson released Nigel's hair, retreating into the mirror. Nigel fell to the ground, his body convulsing and blood spurting out of the slit in his neck. Nate knelt beside him, pressing his fingers against the cut, trying to stop the blood flow.

Nigel made sick gurgling sounds, choking on his own blood. He stared at Nate desperately, grabbing his wrist, repeating the same thing over and over again: "I don't wanna die, I don't wanna die, I don't wanna die…"

Nate grabbed a nearby towel and pressed it against his neck. "Hold on, Nigel, hold on!"

William gripped his mutilated stomach, gagging. "He's killed again," he coughed, tears rolling down his face. "The Doctor's killed again."

All of the tension slowly went out of Nigel's body and his hand lost its grip on Nate's wrist. His knuckles hit the linoleum floor with a dull thud.

"No," Nate felt tears welling up in his eyes and one slid down his cheek. "No, you son of a bitch!" he yelled, grabbing Nigel's pistol and throwing it at the mirror, shattering it.

———— End Part 3 ————

Part 4: It's Always Darkest Before Dawn

Chapter 14

Nigel's glassy eyes stared ahead of him at nothing, his mouth hanging limply open, blood running down one side of his chin. Nate sniffed back his tears, glaring down at the broken glass on the floor. He glanced up at Nigel, but quickly returned to glaring down at the shards of glass. His blonde hair, all the blood... It brought back memories of Mary, a deep cut running the length of her torso, coughing up blood.

"I couldn't save her either," he said under his breath, burying his face in his hands.

William grabbed Dean's shoulder, causing him to jump. His hand was covered in green gunk and blood. "I'm not crazy..." he struggled to say, gagging. "It's the key... the key." He coughed, closing his eyes and turning away, removing his grody hand from Dean's shoulder. His chest stilled. Dean turned to Nate squatting on the ground, his face in his hands, rocking back and forth over the shattered glass by Nigel's corpse.

"Nate." He walked over to him. "Nate." He grabbed his forearm and his hands fell away from his face, but he continued to stare at the floor. "I don't think Redmoor's doing too well."

Nate slowly turned to look at him, but his eyes were distant. "He was always there for me..." he said as if he was not talking to anyone in particular. "But he called my name and I didn't answer him... I didn't answer him!" he raised his voice.

Dean grabbed him by his shirt collar, shaking him. "Come on man, snap out of it. What happened wasn't your fault," he looked back over his shoulder at William. "But I'm not the doctor here. I can't help him."

Nate slowly stood and walked over to William. He lay perfectly still, his head turned to the side, his eyes closed as if asleep. Both of his hands rested on his mangled stomach, his fingers covered in red blood and green muck. Nate put his ear to William's chest. He stood, looking at Dean, shaking his head.

"Rest in peace." He said, looking down at William's tranquil face.

"Poor bastard," Dean shook his head sadly as Nate knelt to the floor to retrieve the relic William had given him. He had dropped it in all of the confusion. It was just like the carving. It had three distinct parts: one semi-centered and the other two branching off jaggedly from it. Each of the three branches ended in a crooked polygon, with line drawings inside. It appeared to be made of a dark ancient stone, such as black granite, and each branch was tipped with a small colored rock: one blue, one orange, and one green. *"It's the key."*

He strapped it to his belt, looking up at Dean. "Kennedy must've still been alive when William saw him… We have to go find him… He said, 'Find the priest. He knows. He knows about the Doctor.'"

Nate turned to exit the kitchen through the doors to the dining hall. "He knew," Dean said suddenly. "He really knew this was going to happen. He knew this was coming. That's why he told us about what happened in the past. To warn us; to prepare us."

Nate looked back at Nigel's body. "He knows more about this than we do... Enough people have died. It's time to end this."

"Why us, Nate?" Dean had not budged. "He told us... Everyone else has died but us. How did he know?"

Nate stared back at him, trying to come up with a good answer. "I don't know." They stared at each other for another long moment. "But we have to find him if we are gonna find out anything... Especially now that Redmoor is gone too."

Dean shook his head. "There must be something more to this, because I know I couldn't have escaped from Richardson on my own. At least not now, the way he is." He slowly followed Nate.

"We aren't very far from the chapel. The dining hall leads out into the courtyard and from there we can-" he hesitated, "-hopefully find him."

As the two made their way out of the dining hall into the courtyard, they covered their eyes, the white snow was blinding compared to the dark sky. As Nate looked up, he could have sworn the clouds had taken on a green hue. The courtyard was dead silent as they walked slowly to the chapel door, trying not to slip on the icy path. Nate and Dean looked at each other before Dean creaked the door open a crack. They both peeked in and saw the Chaplain bent over the offering table, his back to the door. He turned his head to the right and the shadow of a smile tugged at the corners of his mouth.

"Ah, it's you."

Both of the young men turned as the Doctor - in his black scrubs with bloody knives hanging from his waist - walked into the small amount of light leaking through the stained glass windows. "You were expecting me?"

"I've known this was coming. I had a feeling. Like that day, with the tragedy in the mines."

The Doctor laughed hoarsely. "That was nothing."

Kennedy ignored the quip at his expense. "And then there was your obsession, Morris. All those years trying to find a way in, even when you took an oath as a doctor to help people. All those sick things you did in the West Wing."

"I had to find her... I was *meant* to find her..." The Doctor looked down at his gloved hands, "And I did."

"Tell me, how does it feel, now that you've been touched by it? Is it like you imagined?"

"Oh, Kennedy... It's so much more than I could've ever dreamed."

Nate and Dean saw severe sorrow in the Chaplain's eyes as he looked at what had once been Dr. Morris P. Richardson. "That poor woman saw you for what you've become."

The Doctor laughed that hoarse laugh again. "Oh yes, scared Abigail Norris. I taught her a thing or two about electroconclusive treatments early this evening."

The sorrow deepened in Kennedy's eyes as he took in what the Doctor had said. He stood straighter, his arms by his sides. The stained glass cast jagged colored shadows across both of their faces.

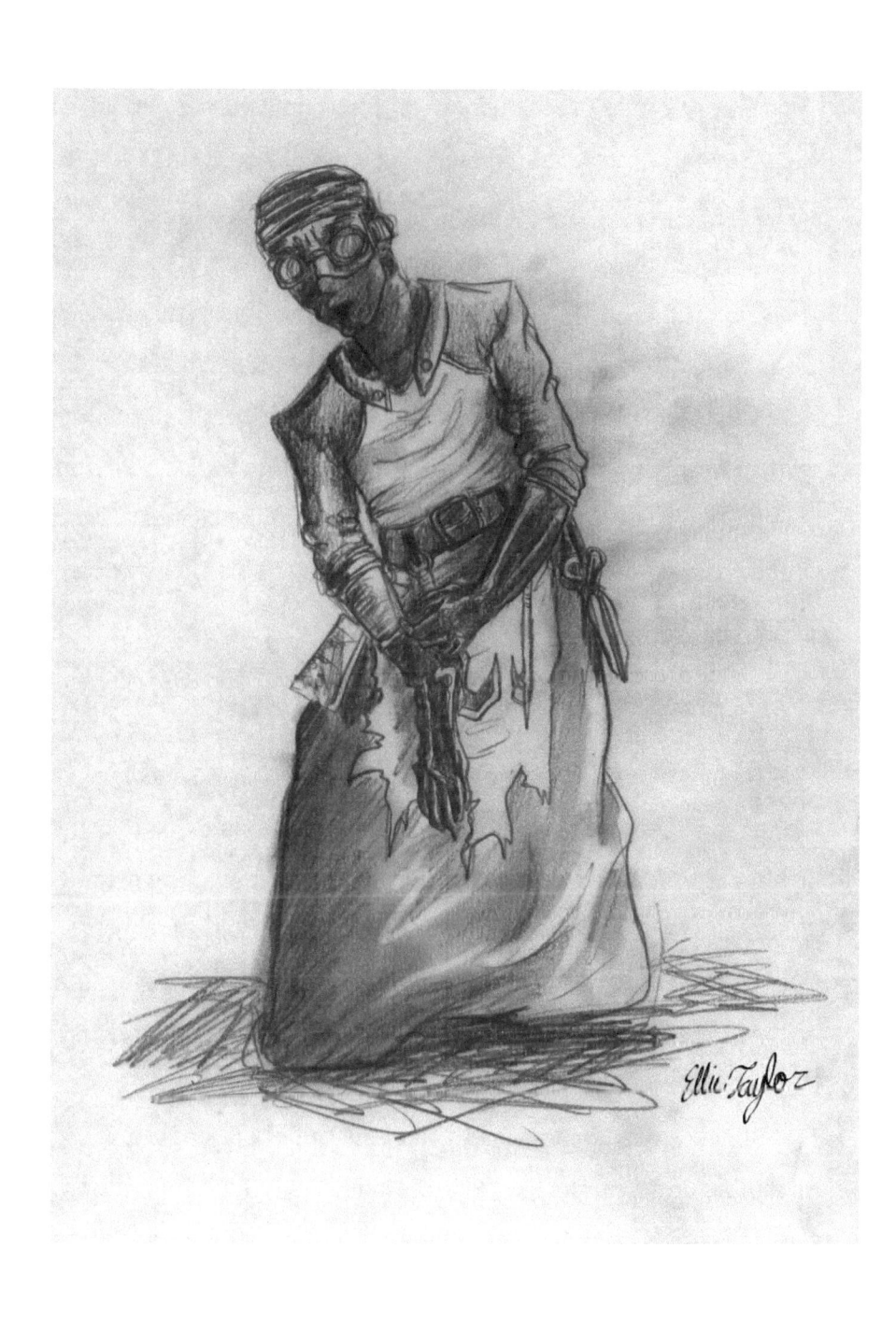
Ellie Taylor

"But you didn't come here to talk... You came here to kill me.

"So you *were* expecting me." Nate could hear a smile in the Doctor's voice that chilled him to the bone.

"I've felt this coming," the Chaplain's small smile reappeared, "and I prepared for it." He glanced over at the door Nate and Dean stood behind so briefly that perhaps he had not looked at all.

The Doctor raised his hand and a chain came from the ceiling, swiftly wrapping around the Chaplain's neck and yanking him up, the sound of his neck breaking echoing throughout the chapel. The end of the chain entered his back and exited through his chest, dripping blood onto the floor.

"No!" Dean cried out, but Nate held him back. The Doctor looked at the door, then vanished.

Dean broke free of Nate's grasp and ran into the sanctuary, stopping just before he reached the hanging Chaplain. Nate had run in after him, but stopped a few pews back, not knowing what to do. Dean stared up at the Chaplain, his mouth slightly agape, his tired eyes rimmed with tears. He slowly fell to his knees, his eyes falling to the growing puddle of blood below the Chaplain, but he seemed to stare right through it.

"I never was a man of faith," he said quietly, a single tear streaming down his cheek, "but this man... My faith in him was the closest I'd ever come to seeing the light. He was so good." His eyes wandered to the offering table where a candle had been overturned due to the Chaplain's sudden departure. Dean stared stupidly at it for a moment before standing up and setting it upright again. Now both candles stood as they should. "We've lost…"

"Two candles…" Nate whispered, and then looked up at Dean. "We have to go on without him."

"What?"

"Didn't you hear him; he said he knew it was coming. Then he looked at us, Dean." He looked down at the relic strapped to his belt. "Two candles - two rays of hope." He felt fear gurgling up in his stomach, trying to make its way up his esophagus, but he thought of Nigel's face and forced it back down.

"Fine," Dean nodded slowly, "but let's search Kennedy's office to see if we can find some answers… Some clues as of what to do."

They entered the Chaplain's office. Everything was as neat and organized as usual. Nate walked over to the file cabinet where the article about the prison had been stored. The drawer was surprisingly empty, containing only a few manila folders stuffed full of documents. Nate retrieved one from the drawer. It contained the yellowed newspaper article and the follow-up article about the prison being shut down.

The next folder was especially fat and the first thing Nate noticed when he opened it was a black and white photograph of a young man, appearing to be in his late twenties or early thirties. There was something strikingly familiar about him. Nate flipped the photo over and read the writing on the back: 'Morris P. Richardson.' A chill ran down Nate's spine. The next paper was a copy of his college degree, stating that he had graduated from Harvard. The other documents were similar: hospital records, lists of patients, the article from when he became the head doctor at Bright Dawn.

The last paper was a handwritten note. Nate read aloud, "I will have to keep an eye on Morris after that last stunt. Granted I have no proof, but there's something I can't shake about him…" Nate flipped back to the old photo. The young Richardson sat in a classic pose, his hand on his chin thoughtfully, looking off past the camera, his large round glasses slightly distorting his face.

"Why do you think he has so many files on Richardson?" Dean shined his flashlight over Nate's shoulder.

"I don't know…" Nate's voice trailed off as he turned to Kennedy's desk and noticed an old-fashioned gramophone sitting right in the middle. It had never been there before. A record sat on it, waiting to be played. Nate looked at the photograph of Richardson one last time before turning on the gramophone and placing the needle appropriately.

The needle scratched across the surface of the vinyl record for a few seconds before Kennedy's voice came out of the horn. "Hello," he cleared his throat. "If you are listening to this, then the chance that the Doctor has reached me is almost certain. I hope it is Dean listening… or Nate. Hopefully both of you have made it this far. I have a lot to explain in an uncertain amount of time. The day that the mines were closed, when all the miners were killed, I had a feeling, a feeling that something was coming. Bright Dawn may seem very institutional - normal. But it indeed is not… I have felt this coming for some time now… But I am sure you are wondering why I chose you of all the people here at Bright Dawn. It is because you two can see past the white walls and defective smiles. You can see there is something dark here, something not right. The wall between our world and the Plane of Anguish is exceptionally thin here, in this small village of Pelf... I don't know how to explain the Plane, only that it is a place of nothing good and it is trying to break through into our world. I chose you two because you have a sensitivity to it, much like me; what some might call a 'psychic sensitivity.'

"Richardson had the sensitivity too... I made the mistake many years ago of confiding in him - telling him of the evils of the Plane. But he was intrigued; something awoke in him that day. A need - a hunger - to seek out and find the Plane, to study it and Malatesta. He stole my book about the Plane... I have no proof, but I know he did. After that, I started keeping better track of my things, sorting and re-sorting. I knew Richardson was started down a dark path and I did everything in my power to steer him away, but he was insistent, almost desperate-"

There was a loud bang on the recording and they heard a chair scraping across the floor as Kennedy stood. Then silence, except for the scratching of the needle.

"Who's there?" Kennedy asked, a slight tremor in his voice.

"Please don't shoot," William Redmoor's voice replied. "I'm not armed... I won't hurt you."

"Come into the light, where I can see you." More silence, then the scraping of a chair as Kennedy sat back down. "Sit down, William. You look awful."

"Those things..." William was breathing heavily and from the sound of his voice, he was crying or close to it. "Father... I want to confess... everything."

"Go ahead, I'm listening."

"I didn't kill my daughter... or my wife... Our daughter, Amanda... must've rolled over in her sleep... or something. I got out of bed to check on her and she wasn't breathing. Then Elizabeth came into the room and when she saw Amanda, she started yelling, repeating the same thing over and over again, 'What did you do to her, William!?' I tried to defend myself, to explain how I'd found Amanda laying there when all of the sudden, in her state of rage, Elizabeth bit me..." William fell silent and quiet sobs could be heard. "And then she wasn't Elizabeth anymore... She was a monster."

"What do you mean 'monster?'"

"Her skin was blue and her eyes weren't right... And she had knives... Her fingers were like daggers. She tried to pick up Amy, to cradle her in her arms, but all she did was rip her up and when I tried to pull her away, she turned on me. I grabbed her wrists, begged her to stop, but she kept thrashing, rippin' herself all up until she grew weak and I let her go and she fell to the floor..." his voice trailed off. "And then she was Elizabeth again, but she was dead and their blood was all over me..." He began to cry again, "That is why I wouldn't speak during the trial; I knew that even if I told the truth, no one would believe me... You probably think I'm crazy too, don't you Father?"

"No."

There was a long silence and Nate was about to switch off the gramophone when William spoke again, "I saw her here... As Elizabeth in the elevator and as that... *witch* in the courtyard... And she's not the only monster. They killed the guards."

"William, I need to ask you something... A while ago, you carved a symbol into one of the clipboards. I need to know what made you draw that... When did you see it?"

"In a dream... It was a horrible dream. I was in this slimy, bloody complex... The skies were filled with green clouds and I could hear screams in the distance, but they were drowned out by roars, roars like nothing I've ever heard. That symbol was some*thing* and since it was the only thing around that looked even remotely like a weapon, I grabbed it and there was a bright flash of light and I woke up."

"William, that place you dreamt of is real..."

"I know it's real... I've heard those roars and I've seen the monsters that I thought were only in my head, here, tonight... Father?"

"Yes?"

"If I die now, now that I finally told someone the truth, do you think I'll get a chance to get into Heaven?"

"If what you say about not murdering your wife and daughter is true, then yes, you definitely have a chance."

"It's spreading, isn't it...?" There was silence and Nate was almost positive that Kennedy had nodded. "This is all my fault... I have to stop it." The sound of footsteps, running across the floor, getting farther away until they completely fading out.

"William! William, come back!" Kennedy cried after him. There was another long silence and then Kennedy sighed heavily before speaking again. "In order to enter the Plane of Anguish, you must do one of two things. The first is to find someone who has experienced an unearthly amount of pain and grief. You will use them as a portal to reach into that world... But before you can enter, you too must experience true anguish. Richardson tried to find a portal for years. He even stooped to shipping in foreigners off death row and experimenting on them in the West Wing. But then there was William, with the pain of the loss of his family, knowing everyone thought him mad, and the physical pain of the surgery. Malatesta reached through him and latched onto what was Dr. Morris P. Richardson." He paused. "All my life I have prepared for this day... But I did not anticipate his - *her* - strength. Richardson is just a pawn now, a puppet of Malatesta..."

He cleared his throat. "The other way into the Plane is known only to me. When they went into the mines, they discovered a sarcophagus of sorts, but could not open it. My father hid it in the church and when I came of age, he made me swear to protect it... It's been here, within this office, the whole time I have lived at Bright Dawn. In the book Richardson stole from me, it spoke of such a portal, a non-human portal. It is locked away in a hidden room in my office, safe from seekers of the Plane like Richardson.

"If this is not ended here; if Malatesta gets out of the Plane, and she and the others get outside this hospital and Pelf... The world as you know it will be over. I place my faith in you, whoever is listening..."

The needle fell off the edge of the record, and it spun aimlessly for a few moments before Dean switched it off.

"The portal is hidden here..." Dean was still taking in everything they had heard. "It's been here the whole time..."

They both started searching the walls for a hidden door; something out of place. Nate noticed a framed newspaper article on the wall that hung slightly crooked, as if it had been moved recently. He walked closer to it and squinted at the small print. It was an obituary dated 'August 9th, 1969' for 'Father Sean Kennedy.' Nate took the frame from the wall and discovered a combination lock set into the wall behind it. But in place of numbers, it had letters so that the combination would spell out a four letter word.

"Dean," Nate called over his shoulder and he appeared with the flashlight. "It's a four letter combination."

"Try 'dead,' that was what the shards spelled in Richardson's office."

The door to the office was suddenly thrown open and the black cloud of smoke that had consumed Keith floated into the room. Dean drew his gun, though the bullets had had no affect before. They were cornered. The relic strapped to Nate's belt began to glow and the creature hissed in agitation. Nate unstrapped it from his belt and held it out toward the creature and it hissed, retreating.

"Figure out the combination," Nate said over his shoulder. "'Dead' didn't work."

Dean knelt to look at the lock and shifted the last letter to an 'N' to spell 'Dean.' Nothing. The relic made a strange humming noise as it glowed. Dean tried 'Nate.' Still nothing. The creature tried to advance, but seemed to be repelled as the relic hummed louder. Dean frowned down at the lock, then an idea struck him. He turned the 'N' to an 'F' and the lock clicked as it spelled the word 'fate.'

"Nate, I figured it out, come on!"

Nate kept the relic raised as he followed Dean into the hidden room and slammed the door shut behind them.

Chapter 15

The room was small and dimly lit by candles, casting eerie shadows on the tribal masks that lined the walls. In the center of the room lay the sarcophagus. Oddly shaped indentations were set in the top surrounded by intricate carvings of spiders, scorpions, and bats. Dean knelt, wedging his fingers into the small gap between the sarcophagus and its lid, grunting as he pulled with all his might, but it would not open.

"He said they couldn't open it… How do *we* open it?" Dean stood, frustrated.

"Do we want to open it?" Nate asked quietly. "Do we want to cross over to that world?"

"You know we have to stop it… No matter what it takes."

"Yes," Nate clenched his jaw, knowing Dean was right. Enough had died already; if it got out of Pelf… No, he could not bring himself to think about that. He noticed the relic was still humming in his hand and when he looked down, the colored rocks still glowed. "*It's the key,*" William's words echoed in his mind.

"I know how to open it," he said suddenly. Before Dean could ask how, he held the relic out over the sarcophagus. It glowed brighter and its three branches became separate parts, landing in their respective spots in the lid of the coffin. The whole room began to glow and Nate knew that they were on what would be their final journey into the Plane of Anguish.

~~~~~~~~~~~~~~~~~~~~~~~~~

The fog had grown so thick that the visibility from the general store windows had gone down to zero. Mosher's freezing corpse lay behind the counter, just out of view. The zombies had tried to get through the door a few times, but after no success and hearing nothing on the other side, they had finally given up. Biff had pulled the chair with the oven closer, though the heat seemed to dwindle by the second.

"Please let them be alive," he thought, looking down at Katie snuggled against his chest, his jacket wrapped around her. *"Please let them get us out of here."*

~~~~~~~~~~~~~~~~~~~~~~~~~~

The metal walls and floors appeared, stained with blood and grease, the sky full of green puffy clouds. The relic reassembled and returned to Nate's hand, silent and no longer glowing. Nate took a deep breath and looked at Dean, who tried to look back reassuringly.

"This is it…" Nate said quietly.

"Yeah." Dean checked to make sure his gun was loaded before saying, "We need to find Richardson and that Malatesta thing. The book said it could only be killed in the deepest reaches of Anguish… Wonder what that meant- hey!" Dean yelled out, suddenly taking off down one of the many corridors.

"Dean, wait!" Nate called after him. "Come back!" But Dean was already gone. He looked around him, a light green fog curling around his ankles, slightly obscuring the view. He spotted a tunnel that seemed darker than the rest. "Deepest reaches of Anguish eh," he said to himself and began down the path.

The air here was nothing like it had been at Bright Dawn; instead of cold it was oppressively hot and humid, Nate's hair sticking to his forehead, the wet thickness of the air becoming so unbearable that he rolled up the sleeves of his shirt.

A sudden snarl from his right in the silence made Nate jump, followed by an evil cackle and Nate turned just in time to see a large ball of green slime flying toward him and moved out of the way, falling to the grimy ground. He heard a sizzling and turned to see that it had melted away part of the chrome floor like a strong acid. A guttural giggle drew Nate's attention to what had launched the slime. What he saw was the strangest monster he had encountered yet. It had no eyes and a mouth of worn down teeth stretched into a big grin. It was the size of a large dog and had four legs: two large back ones and two smaller front ones to keep it from falling forward. It had a tail-like appendage that curled up along its back, facing forward and ending in a large opening rimmed with more green slime; Nate assumed that was where the ball of muck had been launched from.

He stood, not taking his eyes off of the thing, it not turning away from him. Nate was sure that this - or something like it - was what had killed William. He could not afford a similar fate. He slowly raised the shotgun. He pumped it and quickly side-stepped to the left to avoid being hit by a slime bomb and fired. The shell hit the thing square in the face, causing it to let out several loud, terrible shrieks before falling on its side, defeated. Nate stood over it a moment, wiping sweat from his brow with the back of his hand.

He turned to continue his journey down the tunnel, but two more of the creatures blocked his path. He began to raise the shotgun, but the relic strapped to his belt began to hum lightly and when he looked down at it, it was just barely glowing. He kept the shotgun raised, but reached down to unstrap it with his free hand. The two 'dogs'

grimaced down at him, giggling amusedly, waiting to see what their prey would do. As he raised the relic, it felt almost weightless. He threw it, and it flew through the air swiftly, cutting straight through the first creature and exiting out its back. Instead of defeated shrieks, it made sick sounds as it slowly fell, gurgling on its own innards. The other snarled, turning toward Nate, but the relic returned like a boomerang, entering the thing's back and cutting through it like the first, returning to Nate's hand. Both creatures lay dead, leaking blood and green pus. Nate undid the first two buttons of his shirt, strapping the relic back onto his belt.

He heard a sound system spring to life and ducked, raising the shotgun, looking around frantically. "Dr. Nate Grimfield," the Doctor's voice came over the loud speaker, "why waste your time? We both know you cannot win." Sweat ran down Nate's face. "Can you feel it, Nate? Pressing down on you like the weight of the world; slowly crushing your soul." The speakers shut off.

Nate continued down the path, feeling weaker with each step, a feeling of dread wrapping its icy fingers around his heart. It was difficult to even breathe in the hot wet air. He looked up at the sky and could have sworn it had grown darker. It reminded him of the shag rugs in Richardson's office: dark, almost black, green.

Nate came to what appeared to be a large clearing, spanning on for what seemed like miles in every direction. He finally fell to his knees, unable to take another step. The oppressive heat - the *anguish* - was just too much. His arms hung by his sides, the shotgun dangling in his limp fingers, and he began to cry.

He abruptly stopped crying when he heard someone walking toward him, dragging their feet on the metal ground. He held his shotgun at the ready, struggling to stand up. He could make out the shape of a lumbering man coming toward him. Keith McDonnell's face was suddenly visible through the fog, but he did not look the same. His brown hair appeared to have fallen out in clumps and there was a mere shadow on his lip where his mustache had been. His eyes were sunken in his skull, his glasses gone, his skin wet and pale with almost a slight blue tint.

He sighed in exasperation, grabbing Nate's shirt to keep from falling. "This… place…" he struggled to say; when he spoke, Nate could see that his teeth had yellowed, "it just takes away… all of your happiness… and hope… It just… It just…"

"Calm down," Nate put his hand on Keith's shoulder, but regretted it when he felt how thin he was. Bone thin. "How did you escape the shadow?"

"It's what brought me here," he groaned, wincing in pain, a few of his teeth cracking. "It sucked me into this place… How did you… get here?"

"It's a long story, here, sit down, you look awful-"

"No," Keith fought to stay standing. "I have to get out of here, we both-" There was a cracking noise and Keith began to cry out in pain. It was followed by a series of cracks and Nate recognized the sound as that of bones breaking. Keith continued to scream and Nate looked down to see Keith's shirt ripping open as his chest split open down the middle, his ribs jutting out on either side.

"No," Nate said, trying to back away, but Keith had Nate's shirt in a vice grip, continuing to scream as his pumping heart was exposed. As his eyes opened just the slightest bit, Nate could see that they were now bright green. "No," he clenched his jaw, his eyes full of sorrow and resolve as he raised the shotgun in front of him, pumping it. "I'm so sorry Keith." He pulled the trigger. Keith's heart burst, blood splattering onto Nate's face and dark shirt. As he fell to the ground, what started as a human cry ended as a gurgling growl.

Nate gritted his teeth, staring down at the body, then rested the shotgun on his shoulder and turned in the direction he had been going, anger and hatred bubbling in his gut.

The speakers sprang to life and the Doctor's voice could be heard again. "Soon the Plane of Anguish will burst through into our world. The sky will blacken, blood will fall like rain, and the air will be filled with the music of pain."

"Not if I can help it," Nate said back, wiping the blood from his face with the back of his hand, his voice filled with renewed determination as the speakers shut off.

Chapter 16

Nate continued down the tunnel, the humidity and Anguish weighing him down, each step more difficult than the last. Yet there seemed to be a force pulling him further down the path, farther into the Plane. He did not know how long he had been walking or how many shotgun shells he had left. He was sure he was nearing the deepest reaches of Anguish. He kept hoping that he would run into Dean, that the whole Plane was a labyrinth leading to this point - that Dean was alive.

Something became faintly visible through the fog and he brushed his sweat-drenched hair out of his eyes. A large building came into view as he drew nearer to it. Large double doors lay before him, slightly resembling the doors to the West Wing. He looked around, gripping the shotgun with both hands.

"Dean!" he yelled out, looking all around, but no response came; no movement in the fog. "Dean…" he repeated, more weakly this time. But he was nowhere nearby… or dead already. Maybe both. Why had he had to run off alone?

Nate turned and gripped the door handle. He noticed a postcard from Paradise sticking out from under the door. It read: "There's no way you can defeat him now. I'm sorry I ever got your hopes up. – William." But the handwriting was not the same as the others had been; probably the Doctor's idea of a sick backhanded joke. He let the postcard fall to the ground and gripped both door handles in his hands, pulling them open.

What he entered was a large square arena, the walls and floors covered in circular carvings filled with strange symbols. The doors slammed closed behind him and he turned, his gun raised.

"You've come far," the Doctor's voice came over the sound system. "I'd always thought you would… Did you think it was luck that brought you here to Bright Dawn? It was destiny Nate; *destiny* brought both of us here. You and I are quite the same. Join me - join Malatesta - while you still have the chance."

Nate gritted his teeth, looking around, trying to figure out where the Doctor's voice was coming from. "I am nothing like you… You're a monster and a murderer… If destiny brought me here, it was to defeat you, not join you."

"You disappoint me Nate. I thought we'd make the perfect team. You and I are like two sides of the *same* coin."

"You are precisely right," Nate chuckled derisively, "complete opposites."

"Well, since I can't seem to make you change your mind," the Doctor's voice no longer came through the speaker, it was close. Nate turned, spotting a dark figure through the fog, which had thinned out a little. "Malatesta, we bring you an offering. Do with him what you will."

The Doctor's whole body glowed and Nate noticed the circular carving he stood in the center of glowed as well. The Doctor vaporized as a large creature emerged from the circle, which appeared to be a portal of some kind. It was as the book had described: an ancient serpent of colossal size, wrapped in chains. As it roared, Nate observed a large pale green gem set back in its throat. It towered over him, looking down at him and he suddenly felt like the smallest creature alive, alone in his fight against this monstrosity.

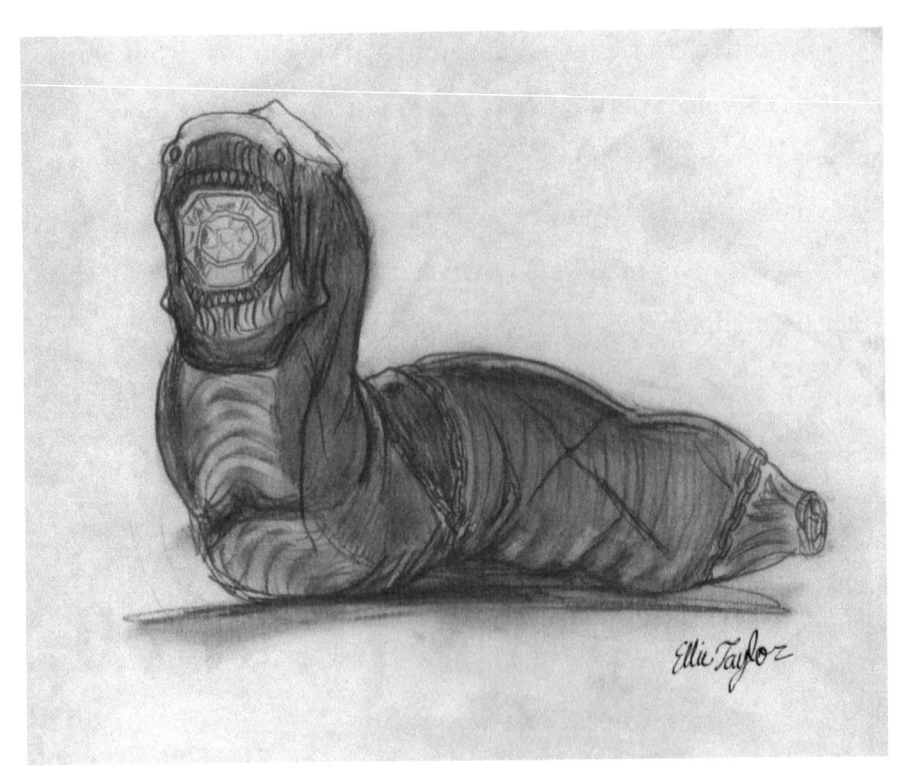

A loud humming and tugging at his belt made him look down to see the relic glowing brighter than it ever had before, pulling at its restraint to his belt as it tried to levitate. Nate's attention was drawn back to Malatesta as she roared again and sank back into the portal, which ceased to glow. He looked around him and spotted a portal on the wall glowing and he ducked just as Malatesta soared out of it, gliding along until she entered a glowing portal in the opposite wall.

"Shit!" Nate shouted as the portal he stood on glowed and he stepped to the side, falling. Malatesta towered over him once more, roaring before releasing a torrent of fireballs at him. He pumped the shotgun and shot her side, and even though she let out a cry, it seemed to have little to no effect. She retreated into her portal and Nate stood, spinning around, waiting to see where she would strike next.

The Doctor's voice came over the speakers again. "Why do you fight when you cannot win?" Nate dodged Malatesta soaring through the air. "Nigel is dead. Keith is dead. William is dead. *Dean* is dead."

"No…" Nate stopped, turning as Malatesta came up out of the portal behind him. "Dean…" Anguish took hold of him for a moment, but then anger: the same anger as when he had tried to stop Nigel's bleeding, the same anger as when he had stood over Keith's body, filled him. "*They* are why I fight!" He turned, pumping the shotgun and as Malatesta roared, exposing the green gem in her mouth, he let out a battle cry and fired. But he was out of range and missed. He yelled again, throwing the shotgun to the ground and unstrapping the relic from his belt, but a fireball knocked him to the ground.

He lay on his back, the air knocked out of him, gripping his burnt chest and shoulder with his free hand. Malatesta leaned over him, waiting to come in for the kill.

"Are you ready to die, Nate? What did this world ever do to deserve such sacrifice?" the Doctor's voice asked mockingly.

Nate looked up into the face of Malatesta - the face of death - when he noticed a dark figure running along the top of the wall that enclosed the arena, and the figure suddenly leapt onto Malatesta, both hands gripping some kind of dagger that it drove into the top of

Malatesta's head. She let out a startled cry of pain, her gem visible once more.

"Now, Nate! Now!" Dean's voice shouted from atop Malatesta's head.

Nate smiled with relief and drew his arm back, flinging the relic into Malatesta's gaping mouth. As it came in contact with the jewel, it shattered. Malatesta let out a defeated, wilting cry and as she began to fall, Dean cried out, losing his balance and falling from her head, the dagger clattering to the ground. As Malatesta hit the ground, causing it to shake, Dean let out an earsplitting cry. Blood began to seep from Malatesta's mouth as Nate ran toward her, looking for Dean. He found him, his leg trapped under the massive worm's body.

"Dean!" Nate said with relief.

"Hey," Dean winced, "my leg is… stuck."

"Nate Grimfield." Nate turned to see the Doctor standing in the center of the room.

"But Malatesta…" Nate said, astonished.

"You may have destroyed her body, but a part of her lives on: in *me*."

"No…" Nate saw a green glow from behind the Doctor's thick goggles and a glimpse of moist rotten blue skin as the Doctor turned his head.

"But I am tired of games. I am going to kill you both right here and now." He approached Nate. "Any last words, Dr. Grimfield?"

Nate stood a moment, looking bewildered. Dean fought to get his leg loose, grunting with exertion.

"There is one thing." Nate looked up at the Doctor. "This," he held up the relic.

"No Nate!" Dean cried out, pulling harder on his leg.

"It isn't from my world and it is very powerful," Nate continued. "If you are going to lead the Plane of Anguish into my world, I think it is only fitting that you have it." He extended his hand that was holding the relic toward the Doctor.

"No Nate, don't give it to him!" Dean shouted adamantly.

The Doctor turned to him. "He doesn't have a choice," he hissed, turning back to Nate and grabbing the relic.

"No…" Dean gave up on his leg, defeated.

"Now that this is in the hands of its rightful owner-" the Doctor stopped speaking abruptly and stared at his hand as the relic began to glow and hum. "What?" He tried to drop it, but it stuck to his hand. "Wait… wait, no! Take it back!" He thrust his arm at Nate.

"I can't," Nate said, his voice and face void of emotion.

"You! You tricked me!" The humming grew louder and the colors glowed more vibrantly. The Doctor shouted, his whole body glowing. "Nooooo!"

There was a bright flash of green light and suddenly Nate and Dean were surrounded by darkness, the cold air hitting their sweaty bodies causing them to cringe.

"We…" Dean said breathlessly, realizing there was no longer any weight on his leg. "We are back at Bright Dawn."

Chapter 17

Nate walked over to Dean, putting Dean's arm around his shoulders and wrapping his arm around Dean's back, helping him to his feet. He cried out as his broken leg was moved, but was soon standing, leaning on Nate for support. "How the hell did you know to give that to him?"

"It was the key," Nate said quietly. "William knew all along."

Dean nodded, still looking perplexed. All of the sudden the lights came back on, blinding them. The forced heat could be heard blowing through the mangled vents around them.

"The power's back on," Nate said.

"Yeah... But we are still locked in," Dean grunted. "We need to get to the main security office... There's an override for the locks there."

They began down the hall they had been returned to at Dean's pace, until they found a stairwell which told them that they were currently on the first floor; they needed to get to the second.

"Elevator," Dean said and they began toward it.

"So why'd you run off like that? Being separated could've gotten us killed."

"To be honest, I was spooked..." Dean took a deep breath. "I saw... Redmoor's kid," he paused, "clear as day... And she took off running down the corridor, so I followed, not wanting to lose sight of her. I ran until I couldn't see her anymore, but I could hear her giggling and when I turned the corner, I could see her lying on this stone altar." They entered the elevator. "But it wasn't her at all... It was this strange doll. I looked up and above her were several chains wrapped around this... this dagger. The chains all jingled and the dagger came loose, landing point down in the doll's chest and blood began to leak out of it. As my fingers wrapped around the handle, it glowed and I could make out these strange symbols carved into the blade... And then I heard you call my name, from far far away. But I heard it." He coughed as they exited the elevator. "And the rest... Well, you were there for the rest."

They entered the security office and Nate lowered Dean into a chair in front of the main computer, and he began typing.

~~~~~~~~~~~~~~~~~~~~~~~~~~

Mosher's old heater sprang to life, the sudden rattling causing both Biff and Katie to start. Biff looked around, then stood and flipped the light switch. The lights came on.

"The power's on," Katie smiled, standing and looking out the window. "The fog is gone! And so are those things!"

Biff walked to the door and slowly opened it, stepping outside, the nail gun in hand. Katie followed him and as they looked out over the lake, the sun began to rise, the first rays of the bright dawn making the snow blinding.

"The sun is rising." Katie hugged Biff and he put his arm around her shoulders.

The lock to the village gate clicked and it came open, exposing the snow-covered road. "Nate, Nigel, and Dean... They made it," Biff smiled.

~~~~~~~~~~~~~~~~~~~~~~~~~~~

Nate rolled Dean out the front doors of Bright Dawn in a wheelchair they had found and unlocked the black company car with the license plate that read 'BRTDWN3.' He helped Dean into the passenger seat and rolled the wheelchair away from the car before climbing behind the wheel and turning it on, cranking up the heat. He shifted into Reverse and the tires peeled out for a moment before gaining traction, and they drove off in the direction of Pelf.

Biff and Katie exited the gate as Nate skidded to a stop and they climbed into the backseat.

"Nate! Dean!" Katie said happily, beaming. Her smile shrank. "Where's Nigel?"

Dean looked at Nate, who stared distantly out the window before replying. "He didn't make it…"

"I'm sorry," Biff said, noting Nate's silence.

Dean turned to Nate again, "Nate?"

He turned back to the wheel, and then nodded slightly. "We need to get to the nearest hospital and police station." He shifted into Drive and sped off, leaving Bright Dawn and Pelf behind them.

───── End Part 4 ─────

Epilogue: William

Epilogue

Nate sat in the armchair in the living room of the two-bedroom flat. The television babbled in the background, noise to avoid the silence. Snow fell quietly outside the window, sunlight leaking in through the blinds. The door opened and Dean walked in on crutches, carrying a few papers.

"Anything interesting on?" Dean asked, glancing at the television.

"Not really watching it," Nate replied, standing and walking over to the small piano in the corner of the room, absently playing a few notes: D, E, A. D, D, E. A, D, D. E, A, D. D, E, A…

"You've been playing that same tune since the incident," Dean sifted through the papers in his hand. "What song is it?"

"Not a song… William used to play it in music therapy… It's what the broken CDs in Richardson's office meant: the notes on the piano are 'D. E. A. D.'"

"Interesting… But why play it? I thought we wanted to put all that behind us." Dean pulled an envelope from the stack. "Look, it's a letter to you from Katie." He handed it to Nate, the return address to Paris, France. "It was nice of you to pay for their trip."

"They needed to get away for a while…"

"It couldn't hurt to take your own advice." Dean leaned on the kitchenette counter. "I'm thinking of moving back to New York myself."

"It's just… hard," Nate stared out the window

209

"This is about Nigel and Mary, isn't it?"

"Yes… and, all of them."

It had been about a week ago that they had been told they could return to Bright Dawn to retrieve their personal belongings. Not that there had been much to retrieve, but Nate had also salvaged Nigel's shattered red flashlight and taken one of the 'Bright Dawn' pens from Mary's desk. He knew it was silly, but it was all that he had left of them.

And then, just a few days after that - when the authorities were not swarming around Bright Dawn - he and Dean had returned to tie up one final loose end. They had retrieved the sarcophagus from the hidden room in Chaplain Kennedy's office and taken it out to the far docks in Pelf and sunk it in the lake, where no one would ever find it.

Nate and Dean's attention was drawn to the television as the news' loud entry played and a young woman behind a desk came onto the screen. Above her left shoulder there was a picture of Bright Dawn.

She began to speak, "It has been nearly two weeks since the patient riot at acclaimed Michigan psychiatric hospital, Bright Dawn Medical Treatment Center, and although most of the staff, patients, and nearby residents affected by the outbreak have been accounted for, there are still a few names among the missing, including the director of the facility, Dr. Morris Richardson. As stated in previous reports, witnesses recounted that when the power went out, the high security patients got out and proceeded to massacre the other patients and staff, a few even finding a way out of the facility and into the neighboring Pelf village, which is now a ghost town. That being said, high security patient William Redmoor is still at large, as no evidence of him dead or alive has been recovered. Redmoor is believed to be possibly armed and very dangerous. If you have any information on the whereabouts of Redmoor, or of the others among the missing, please call the number on your screen." A phone number was displayed along with a list of those missing, Keith McDonnell's name among them.

The four of them had agreed in the car to tell a story about how the prisoners had broken containment and killed almost everyone in the hospital and village. It was easier than telling what had really happened. Like William had said, no one would believe them. It was just too farfetched and they had no evidence, the remains of the creatures had been destroyed along with the Plane.

"That still bugs me," Dean said quietly.

"Hm?" Nate turned to him.

"William… He was dead, we left the body in the kitchen, I even told the police that when they questioned us… But they found nothing, not even traces of his blood… I don't know how that's possible."

"As for Bright Dawn's future," the news anchor continued, "authorities have announced that it will not be re-opened, due to its violent history and this most recent incident. Some rumors have leaked about the building being condemned, but as of now there is no confirmation of that. And now we bring you our weekly forecast, Albert…"

"It is strange… But so are a lot of the things we experienced that night." Nate sat back down in the armchair.

"True… But there is still just something wrong about it…" Dean grabbed a beer out of the fridge.

"They won't find Richardson… or Keith… They're gone, with the Plane and its monsters," Nate said quietly, staring blankly at the television.

Dean nodded, taking a swig of his beer, then frowned thoughtfully, slowly taking the bottle from his lips. "What if William just… disappeared too?"

Nate mulled this over for a moment and it made a frightening amount of sense: William had been touched by the Plane long before he had arrived in Pelf and had set Malatesta's plan in motion; he had been her gateway to enter Richardson and our world.

"I guess we'll never know," he replied, standing and pouring himself something stronger than a beer.

---- End ----

About the Author

Sarah J Dhue is a fiction author from Illinois and has been writing since she was in elementary school. In addition to books, she also writes poetry, short stories, and songs. She loves networking with other writers - and artists of other media - and runs a writing group that meets weekly at her local coffee shop. Some of her other interests include coffee, photography, graphic design, social media, animals, art, travel, and music. Sarah currently resides with her family and cats in southern Illinois.

To learn more about Sarah, visit sarahjdhuephotos.com